I0598007

Arden Mercer's wife Marilyn didn't turn out to be the person he thought she was. So when tragedy strikes and Marilyn is killed, Arden doesn't know what to feel. But local law enforcement seems to think Arden had a hand in his wife's death. When the accusations start to fly Arden's best friends, Nevers and Sally, pull together the best of the best to get to the bottom of the biggest Lake Charles scandal in years. With information coming in from places like Tucson, Arizona and New York City, Arden and his friends have to move fast. If they can't find out what Marilyn was up to, it could mean Arden will be sleeping on a poly-blend sheet for the rest of his life.

Alligator Shoes

Melissa Ward Anderson

Copyright Year: 2006
Copyright Notice: by Melissa Ward Anderson. All rights
reserved.

Cover Photo © 2006 by Melissa Ward Anderson

Photograph of Author © 2005 by Melissa Ward
Anderson

ISBN: 978-0-6151-3510-6

Don't do it because you think you deserve it.
Do it because you can.
-James T. Anderson II

Back Where We Started

*I remember the day vividly. We were making our way to
Nantucket aboard the Flying Cloud; acting like we were
rich people. Arden was sitting across from me looking
so young and totally in his element. His green eyes were
so clear; his blonde hair had been tousled by the wind
outside. I'm sure he thought he was dressed down, but
he looked fabulous, as always. He'd taken off the
sweater he had been wearing with his khaki pants and
threw it casually over his shoulders, revealing a
sparkling white t-shirt. He smiled at Sally and I and we
knew he was happy. We all were. This was before
Arden accused me of being a baby, and I accused him of
hanging around with a Yankee slut.*

*Not long after we settled in for the ride to Nantucket,
Sally fell asleep, her brown bob perfectly framing her
face. Her long lashes brushed her cheeks as she slept. I
was always so jealous of her lashes, but Sally said she'd
rather have my eyes with no lashes at all. She's full of
crap. She has the prettiest brown eyes I've ever seen.
While Sally slept I tried to get the lowdown on Marilyn,
Arden's new love-interest. At the time, Marilyn was
some kind of creative consultant working for the
company which published the book Arden and I wrote
together. I wasn't crazy about her, but for Arden's sake
I gave it my best shot. Marilyn told us about growing up
in New York. She said her parents were teachers and
that's what prompted her to get an English degree. But
she took it in another direction, heading into the
publishing world. I wasn't sure about Marilyn. I was
trusting Arden's judgment at that point; I didn't have
any reason not to. As I look back on that day now, I
realized just how innocent we all were. I mean, we were
rotten, don't get me wrong, but as Rick Springfield
would say, success hadn't spoiled us yet.*

I tried very hard to get the bitch in my brain to go away, but it just wasn't working. I was raised well enough to know that I had to be nice on the outside, but manners don't work when it comes to stray thoughts. Manners will flee fast when you see someone walking down the street, belly hanging over the low-riding jeans, shirt cut to showcase the boobs. That's when the bitch in your brain takes over and says, "Did she look in the mirror before she left the house?"

So to be honest, I wasn't paying much attention to what Marilyn was saying, which wouldn't make much of a difference in the long run, being that she was lying like a rug. Or maybe like a shag carpet, all matted and tacky. And really, I was trying; benefit of the doubt and all. I just think that women are the best judges of other women. We make huge mistakes with men. There's documentation of that. But other women? We can see right through them because we all have the same doubts, they just manifest themselves in different ways. And that was the thing I couldn't put my finger on. I figured Marilyn for having an agenda; I just didn't know what it was. Later, when Sally and I discussed it, she confessed to feeling the same way. But we put it aside for a long time. We wanted Arden to be happy. For the first time in a long time, Sally and I kept our mouths shut. Trust me, it won't happen again.

Nevers

I can remember when I was little, sitting at the counter in the kitchen reading about Jean Lafitte in the *Pirates Pantry Cookbook*, put out by the Junior League of Lake Charles. I loved the fact that Lake Charles had such a colorful history; pirates and warships and treasure at the bottom of the bayous and waterways. I used to dream of diving under the murky water while swimming in Big Lake and surfacing with handfuls of gold doubloons, my nose streaked with white zinc; a victorious grin on my face.

It is well documented, of course, that in the 1800's, the pirate Jean Lafitte did big business on the Calcasieu River and in Lake Charles. It seems the Buccaneer was respected and regarded as a powerful man. Lafitte was cultured, and according to legend, spoke four languages. Which made sense, in the business he was in. Many people tell stories about his wealth and the fact that he buried enormous treasures in and around the murky swamps that surrounded the Lake Charles area. And for decades people have searched for the treasure, to no avail. Does that mean that it isn't buried there? Nope. It just means that no one has found it.

And the residents of Lake Charles love this. In fact, every year we throw a huge party in Jean Lafitte's honor. Imagine celebrating a pirate, a swindler. But this is what we do; Contraband Days is a week long shindig in the spring where people get out on their boats and act like pirates, drinking and playing hard. It is a celebration of debauchery, of the pirate lifestyle. The fashion scene during Contraband Days is a whole different story. And it's something the city doesn't advertise in brochures. Think tube tops and flip flops...On someone's Maw Maw.

I tell this story because we discovered a pirate in our midst, quite by accident. We were being swindled and we didn't even know it. And it hit everyone, me, Stewart, Sally, Arden. It hit Arden the worst, like a sucker punch to the back of the head. And it all started with a phone call.

It was late in the afternoon when the phone rang. I was dozing on the couch on the screen porch that faced the back yard. The front porch was still my favorite, but after my surgery I relocated because of the street noise. Stewart had done an incredible job with the landscaping, roses and banana trees all along the border, and camellia bushes right outside the back door. Of course we had to enlist the help of Miss Lou Dubois when it came to the roses; she's an expert inside and outside of the home. At the center of the plush green yard was yet another swing for us to enjoy and a gorgeous wood patio set from Restoration Hardware with six chairs, as we were always having company.

At first I couldn't figure out what the sound was. I stirred and looked at the television for what seemed like an hour before the phone rang again and I was jolted fully awake by its obnoxious tone. I began to search for it frantically, yet carefully, and found it in what we had come to call "the big green chair" after only one more ring.

"Nevers, it's Arden…Something terrible has happened."

And this is how it went. Arden was frantic, talking fast and scaring me to death. At some point I realized what he was saying to me and I fell back into the couch, knocking over a big glass of iced tea which had been sitting on the floor next to the couch, and sat there watching it be absorbed by the ancient Persian rug that Stewart had inherited from his grandmother. I felt bad, but I couldn't move to stop it; Stewart would just have to understand.

At some point a deputy from the sheriff's office got on the line and asked me if I would be able to come and get Arden, as they were dealing with an outdoor scene and couldn't spare anyone to take him home. Ah, the joys of small town life. I promised I would be there as fast as I could and reluctantly hung up to find my husband.

Stewart was out in the garage, working on his latest project; a boat. He'd taken up fishing and loved being out on the water; I kept teasing him that he was a real southerner at heart; it just took me getting him here for him to realize it. I explained what was going on and that I had to go now because Arden was in total shock. And he said without hesitation, "Get a move on, girl."

I climbed in my Mini Cooper convertible, which Stewart had given me before we got married, and he kissed me goodbye and said he loved me and to be careful. "Yes, sir," I responded. I reversed out of the driveway and eased onto Shell Beach Drive. Heading north to I-10, I decided I should call Sally and let her know what was going on. So I plugged in my hands free cell phone crap and dialed her number.

"Tragedy has struck again," I said when she answered.
"Not Stewart?" she asked nervously.
"No, it's Arden. And Sally, it's a mess."

Then I proceeded to tell her the story.

It was a gorgeous morning. April always brought about warmer days, with cloudless, unending blue skies. And trust me, when the landscape is as flat as it is in Louisiana, sometimes you feel like you can see to forever. Apparently Marilyn and Arden had awoken around nine, and while reading the paper, Marilyn asked about seeing some sights, could they get out and enjoy the day, she wanted to know.

For the better part of the last year, Arden and Marilyn had been globetrotting, following up on Marilyn's screenplay which she had sold to Fox for a "fortune" Arden said. There were rewrites which had to be done, and meetings with producers, and they often found themselves on location for the movie, surrounded by real stars. Arden was not all that impressed, but he said Marilyn would act like a school girl, "ooohing and aahhhing over all of them."

They would find themselves back in Lake Charles for a week here and there, and Arden would insist on spending that time with his Mama and his friends. At first it wasn't a big deal to Marilyn, but eventually she started begging off, claiming jet-lag, or some other kind of bullshit.

So that morning, when she actually wanted to get out and see some of the south, Arden was all for it. He said they could drive down to Hackberry and then further south to Holly Beach (a.k.a. the Cajun Riviera), and Marilyn had agreed, saying she'd read about the Creole Nature Trail and wanted to see the real alligators.

Arden went back to the bedroom to get dressed; excited about their adventure. He chose a pair of Ralph Lauren khaki shorts and threw on an old t-shirt, grabbed a sweatshirt out of the back of the closet, something he only wore when necessary, and found a pair of old, white leather K-Swiss tennis shoes that he probably hadn't worn since high school.

Marilyn was dressed in similar fashion except that she insisted on wearing a pair of Jimmy Choo slides that she picked up in LA. Arden told her it was a foolish decision because they were going to be outdoors, but she wouldn't hear of it. "They are comfortable and I'm wearing them," was her reply. Arden found it hard to argue with Marilyn because (from what she told him) as a child she didn't have much by way of material items, and he eventually dropped the subject.

They filled their Crate and Barrel coffee mugs with Community Coffee and headed out the back door. They drove west on I-10, the same direction I was now going, got off in Sulphur and started going south. Highway 27 is, to me, a historical two-lane thoroughfare. Want to see how the working class really lives? Take highway 27 South. There are homes and small businesses lining the route for several miles, little signs selling veggies. Then you get to areas where there is nothing, nothing but land and water, and you can feel the air change because of the proximity of the Gulf.

If you have to stop, talk to the people. They are like no others you will ever meet. My cousin May and I had to find a place to get string one time when we were on a crabbing trip. It was the adventure of a lifetime. The old man told me I looked pregnant and 40, and May almost fell off the ramshackle dock where his "business" was housed because she was laughing so hard. I was about 22 at the time. And needless to say I didn't find it as funny as May did.

So this is where Arden and Marilyn were headed; a place where people still shrimped and crabbed and fished for a living. They stopped a couple of times before they got to the Creole Nature Trail; Arden wanted Marilyn to appreciate the vastness of the land and understand what it was to grow up in a place like Louisiana; he told her stories about crabbing trips that involved me and Sally, and about being on his uncle's shrimping boat, all these adventures which shaped his childhood. The stories were important to him; he wanted her to understand. Marilyn looked as if she was interested, and when Arden felt like she understood, he drove on.

They got to the Creole Nature Trail around noon. Now, there are no fences at the Creole Nature Trail. And there are alligators there, and rabbits and armadillos and all kinds of other creatures; herons and other birds continually take flight from well hidden places and can scare you to death, so you always want to be on your toes when you are there. Arden explained all of this to Marilyn as they stared walking the paved path.

There had been a few other cars in the parking lot, but they didn't see anyone around. The path was a long and twisting one, and other tourists could have been anywhere. Marilyn began to get antsy after only fifteen minutes or so. She wanted to see the alligators, but they hadn't come across one yet. And then they rounded another bend, and there, very close to the edge of the water, were three baby alligators, nestled in the grass, very close to the water.

Marilyn started to get close. She wasn't scared because the little ones were only about a foot long. Arden told her repeatedly to stay away from them, but she wasn't listening. At one point he grabbed her arm and tried to pull her back. She still had one foot on the pavement and one in the grass at that moment, and as she tried to twist her arm free, she lost her footing on the pavement ("because of those fucking couture slides," said Arden), and landed flat on her ass in the grass only inches away from the little gators.

She was sitting up facing the water, the little gators between her legs, and for a moment, Arden thought everything was okay; Marilyn sort of laughed, and tried to get up. And that's when they both realized that her right foot was caught. Arden thought it was hung up on some reeds at the bank of the water, he reached for her hand, yelling at her to grab on to him, but Marilyn was complaining that she couldn't find her right shoe.

"I'll buy you some new goddamned shoes'" he swore, all the while trying to find something behind him to hold on to in order to pull her back up onto the path. And then he felt the jerk. He lost hold of Marilyn's hand and looked over in shock as she was dragged into the water. He said it happened so quick that he didn't have time to respond. He watched in disbelief as the gator took her under and the "death roll" began. There was nothing he could do. There wasn't a limb he could grab; he thought about pulling her out by the hair, but he couldn't see that either, she was far below in the murky dark water. He didn't know how long he stood there, but eventually he started screaming. A family on vacation from Tucson, Arizona heard his screams and notified the authorities; but not before getting the hell out of there.

"Someone called 911, and when Arden calmed down he called me," I told Sally. It was still unbelievable to me.

"This is way out there, Nevers. I've lived here all of my life and never heard of something like this happening. Oh my God, poor Arden. To have to watch and not be able to do anything about it. Oh, God, he is really going to be a tragic mess. And Marilyn. Poor, poor Marilyn."

Sally had nailed it. Or so we thought.

I turned on some Cake, *Wheels*, to be exact, and smashed down the accelerator with my Old Navy flip flop.

Sally

Good God, I thought. *What have we not been through over the last year?* When Nevers called me on her way to Hackberry, I listened slack-jawed, and disbelieving. Was it not enough that we had to watch Muffy go flying over that bench in Nantucket? And poor Arden. He was so enamored of Marilyn. What would happen now?

I must admit, however, that I wasn't as saddened as I thought I should be. Perhaps it had to do with Marilyn's attitude over the last year. Nevers and I liked her well enough, but, God she could be a bitch to Arden; and to the rest of us in subtle ways. But Arden got the brunt of it. What surprised us was that Marilyn had been so sweet in Nantucket, putting up with Nevers's insecurity, and the drama of Muffy's untimely demise. It was only after she and Arden returned from their first trip to Los Angeles, the night of Nevers and Stewart's engagement party, that I noticed something in her that I thought I'd seen a little of before, and yet I couldn't put my finger on it.

That night...we were having a good time, for the most part. I couldn't drink, and Nevers, although happy was still upset that Arden wasn't there. We had talked about it a little, but with so many people and so much going on, the topic kind of got lost in the shuffle. Nevers had fixed herself a drink and walked across the street to the wharf while I helped her Mama with the food. It was a surprise to all of us when Arden and Marilyn pulled up. I ran over to hug him and he held me tight and whispered, "Make sure that baby knows his uncle Arden loves him."

"How do you know it's a boy?" I asked.
"It's that Cajun blood in me. I just know."

"Well, thanks for blowing the surprise," I said, jokingly. Arden knew what I knew, and had felt since I started to show. It *was* a boy.

"Where is she?"

"She's out on the wharf. And Arden, don't be hard on her. She had a lot to figure out, but she's done it, and without too much drama, I might add. So don't dredge up anything unpleasant. Let's just continue to celebrate."

"Ah, Sally. It's all about the party with you, isn't it?" he said with a wink.

"You know it." And then I watched him walk away. I thought it would be a good idea to find Marilyn and make her feel welcome because she really didn't know anyone. I found her talking to Stewart, and I hung back so I could listen in.

"You really like it here?" Marilyn asked, sounding annoyed

"Are you kidding?" asked Stewart. "This place is like nothing else I've ever experienced. It's like Nantucket in a way, but then again it's not. The rich people and the not so rich people here all hang out together and none of that social-status shit flies, you know what I mean? It's like, as long as you have drinking money, you fit in. As Nevers and them say, 'Welcome to life on the Cajun Riviera.'"

"But don't you miss New York, even a little? I mean, what could you possibly have in common with these people?"

"Marilyn, 'these people' are just like me and you. Hell, Arden is one of 'these people.' What's there not to like?" asked Stewart.

"Well, they talk different," complained Marilyn, "and it drives me nuts when they have to tell a ten-minute story to answer a simple question."

"Well, I love it. The people, the air, the houses, everything feels rich down here. And I don't mean money-wise, I mean fuller, more interesting. I don't ever plan on leaving."

You go, Stewart, I thought. I knew that he had been the right man for Nevers all along. She knew it too; it just took her a while to accept it. I never had doubts about Stewart. But Marilyn, on the other hand, her I doubted. Way in the back of my head, buried very deep, had been that little voice saying: *watch out for that one*. After hearing her exchange with Stewart, the little voice got a little louder. I didn't want to feel that way about her; Arden loved her, so I knew, deep down inside, that there had to be *something* good in her. I just didn't feel like looking for it. And I didn't have to, because not long after her little conversation with Stewart, Nevers and Arden came walking up from the front of the house, hand in hand, looking totally at peace with each other; it was like everything they'd put each other through was buried and gone. The look on Marilyn's face, however, was far from peaceful.

And that is when we really started to see a side of Marilyn that Nevers and I didn't like one bit. Almost exactly a month later Nevers and Stewart got married. They did it quick because Stewart didn't have any family to invite, and Nevers was scared to death that she'd chicken out, not because she didn't love Stewart, but because it was in her nature. We were so excited. We searched high and low to find Nevers her beautiful empire-waist gown, and we planned a simple, but tasteful wedding in no time.

Nevers wanted all garden roses, and everyone in town with a rose garden chipped in. She made her own arrangements, but that was okay. Perfectionist that she is, no one would have done it to her standards anyway. She got a little help from Pierre, but I think that was just an excuse to go to New Orleans and stay at the Monteleone. Of course while we were there we had to go to Orient Expressed on Magazine Street and purchase baby clothes. It only took us about three hours to decide what we wanted; all those gorgeous smocked dresses and outfits…we spent a fortune. But I digress. A couple of days before the wedding, Marilyn got called back to L.A. She was adamant that Arden come with her, but Arden was giving Nevers away and told Marilyn there was no way he was walking away from his duties.

He didn't say much else to us, but the day of the wedding, Arden walked Nevers down the aisle, and Marilyn was no where in sight. Only later, when he was a little drunk did he admit that Marilyn had flown off without him, pissed because he wasn't supporting her. Nevers and I were astonished. It was okay that Marilyn wasn't there, but why did she have to be such a bitch to Arden? He stayed behind because his best friend was getting married and he had the honor of giving her away, not because he didn't want to be with Marilyn. In fact, he left two days after the wedding to meet her sorry ass. I didn't even want to think about that reunion. And so it went for the last year. Marilyn having to leave at a moments notice and Arden trailing after her.

It wasn't great when they were in Lake Charles, either. Arden was always so glad to be home, but I guess the south didn't hold all that much appeal for Marilyn. And we tried. Every time they came home, either Nevers or I would have some kind of dinner party so we could all catch up. Arden was so excited about the baby, and couldn't wait to be there when he was born. And that brought even more undesirable looks from Marilyn.

"This is weird," said Nevers one night after one of our welcome home dinners; we were standing in her kitchen doing dishes. "I mean, I don't think she's jealous, but there is definitely something going on."

"I think that she is just pissed because Arden is so excited. She doesn't do a damn thing to make that boy happy, always barking orders and pulling him away from his Mama and us. I keep waiting for him to get sick of it, but he never loses control with her," I said.

"Which is even weirder because you know he always had words for me and you when we drove him crazy. Maybe he thinks he made a mistake, but doesn't want to fess up to it."

"That could be true. But, Nevers, how long is he going to keep this shit up? He knows that we are all getting tired of her attitude. When is he going to say 'enough is enough'?"

"Hopefully soon," she said with a weary, and very audible sigh.

And something did change. We never knew what happened, but by the time the baby was born, Marilyn was acting like a sane person again. She and Arden were present for the birth, bearing tons of gifts for the baby and me. I delivered in late October and Arden just smiled when they told him I'd had a boy.

So I had my baby, Jackson Aucoin, and after a big christening at the Cathedral, I settled into motherhood. It was interesting to say the least, but Jack and I were having fun. And when Arden was home we would all get together with the baby in tow and you could just tell he was overjoyed. Marilyn never accompanied him on those days, even if she was in Lake Charles. She had started claiming "jetlag" and we let her. I mean who really wants someone like that around their baby? And there were conversations that took place on those days that we never even thought about until after the accident. Conversations about family and heritage and what they meant to us now that we had a child of our own. There was one conversation that proved quite important in retrospect. It was the day that Nevers asked about Marilyn's parents.

"You know, it seems weird now, to say it out loud, but I've never met them, never even talked to them," said Arden.

"That is weird, Arden. I mean I know she's not southern, so you don't get the whole family gathering on the first date, but I can't believe you've never even talked to them," I said.

"It does seem kind of bizarre," Nevers added.

"Well, she talks to them, and when she gets off the phone she says that they send their hellos and all that crap. Should I ask to talk to them? Apparently they are quite studious people, maybe that is just their way. Shit, now y'all have me worrying about this."

"Don't worry about it," said Nevers. "It's just, well; I cannot imagine not wanting to at least hear the voice of the man who marries my daughter, you know, if I had one. But who are we to judge?"

"Exactly. That has gotten us into more trouble than I care to admit, judging people, that is. If Marilyn is okay with it, then we should be too," I said. But I guess we should have questioned it a little more.

Arden

Ever wish you could go back in your life and change something? I know I've wanted to. But not a whole lot of people can admit it out loud. I could never have told Sally and Nevers that I thought I made a mistake, especially when I realized that I'd made it. It was too soon after. Whether we admit it or not, Nevers and I were so caught up in what was going on in our lives that we didn't stop to think about too much. She thanks me now for leaving her, because she feels like she gave attention to areas of her life that would otherwise have suffered. I wish that someone would have given me that opportunity.

When I first met Marilyn I admit I was smitten. All blond and voluptuous, built sort of like Nevers, all curvy. But Marilyn wasn't Nevers. Marilyn was as far from Nevers as you could get, and at that point, I wanted to get far. For years Nevers and I had been so dependent on each other that if someone didn't do something, we were going to grow old and gray together, wondering what our lives could have been, wondering if we would have ever found that one person who would have truly made us complete. And we would have been resentful, blaming each other for the way things turned out. It wasn't an easy decision to make, but when Marilyn flashed that pitiful, you-are-my-guardian-angel-face, saying that she desperately needed someone to go to L.A. with her, well, how could I say no?

I mean I guess I could have just spit it out, but I was so taken with her. And there was a part of me that wanted to get away from Nevers and all the drama we'd created in our lives, so I hopped on that plane and didn't look back. I planned to come home eventually, I just didn't know when. And then I really started to get to know

Marilyn and thought maybe now was better than later. It wasn't immediate; her real persona didn't come out until after the first meeting with the studio people.

"Those fucking cocksuckers, they are gonna throw a couple of million my way for this piece of crap!" she said excitedly.

"Really, Marilyn, is all of that language necessary?" I asked.

"Don't be such a fucking prude, Arden. It isn't like Nevers doesn't cuss. Or does it sound like honey coming out of her mouth?"

"That's uncalled for Marilyn. What is your problem with Nevers anyway?"

"She ran your fucking life, that's my problem with Nevers. She ran your fucking life and she made sure I knew it."

"She does not, nor has she ever, run my life, Marilyn. I don't know where you get that. Because if she did, I wouldn't be here with you."

Marilyn thought long and hard about that one. She knew it was true. And just like some strange creature from a horror movie, she became all sweet again, sitting on my lap and apologizing for the things that she'd said, eventually kissing my neck and whispering in my ear that she loved me. It was a ploy as old as time itself, but I fell for it anyway. As far as sex goes, she was the best thing, the most addictive thing I'd ever experienced in my life. And I must admit it was a little scary. I ended up discovering that Marilyn was like a triangle. One side of her was the sweetest thing you'd ever come across, one side of her was the filthy-mouth bitch, who wasn't a whole lot of fun to be in the room with, and the third side was the sexual side; the side that made you wonder what she'd been up to in her previous lives.

And in the middle of the triangle was all of it. It was like the Magic 8 Ball, shake it up and see what you get. I tried not to shake things up too much. For the most part we were happy. Marilyn might get a little out of whack when we met with the studio people, but I think that was more a power trip than anything. It was after a week with especially-nice-Marilyn that we decided to run off to Vegas and get married. She had actually been sitting on top of me, doing what she does best, when she brought it up. I think that it had to do with the passion, my saying yes, over and over, but it ended up being the answer she was looking for. And just like that we're in the Chanel Boutique at Neiman's in the Fashion Show mall, buying the dress. I guess I should have called Nevers then, but I just couldn't bring myself to do it. And, really, I was having fun. When things were good, they were very good.

And then some guy came to see me one day, out of the blue, just sauntered up to the door. A big, tank of a guy wearing a charcoal suit, with a terrible tie and bad shoes knocked on the door of the bungalow we were staying in at the Beverly Hills Hotel.

"Are you Arden Mercer?" he asked.

"Who wants to know?"

"I work for a certain party who shall remain nameless," was the goons reply.

"What's with all this cryptic shit? Who the hell are you?"

And his tough guy façade faded. "I work for Lyle Gugino."

"Why the hell is Lyle looking for me?" I asked. Lyle was the man that Stewart had sold his family's company to, a man of means, which explained the goon, but it didn't explain why.

"Look, I was just told to find you. You are Arden Mercer, right?"

"Guilty. What are you supposed to do when you find me?"

"I'm supposed to give you this," he said, handing me an envelope.

"Well, now you have."

"Yes, I have. Sorry for the interruption, I'm just doing my job."

"Understood," I said, calming down a little.

I took the envelope back inside and sat down to read it. It was from Stewart, and it was just as classy as he is. He and Nevers were getting married and he wanted me and Marilyn to come home for the engagement party. He said that Nevers had been doing so well, but that he knew she really missed me, and that the Carrie dreams had stopped, and that even though she was doing well, she wasn't the same old Nevers. He included the date and time of the party and I immediately sat down to call the airlines.

I didn't even think to ask Marilyn. That was a mistake. Obviously, where I come from people who love their friends do things for them, try to make them happy because, face it, how many times have they made you happy? But in Marilyn's world, that just wasn't the case. She never really had any friends, so she didn't understand the need to run off to see mine. It took four hours of shopping on Rodeo Drive, at my expense, to make her understand. So that morning, that beautiful morning when my wife asked me to take her somewhere she'd never been, a place that I felt was a part of me, I was overjoyed; maybe there was hope for my marriage.

Flashback

After I filled Sally in on what was going on I got to thinking. She was right; we'd been through so much already, I began to wonder just how much more we could take. But then I always think that, and we always come out okay.

It had started with Arden's emotional homecoming. There I was sitting all alone on the night of my engagement party, about to become a member of a permanent couple, and I had never felt so alone in my life. Arden was my ghost limb, and I needed him back. It was only later that I found out that Stewart had put in a call to Gavin and Gavin had finally given up Arden and Marilyn's location.

And knowing Arden the way I did, I knew when I looked at him that night that things were not going as planned, something was off, even though I couldn't put my finger on it. Sally and I had discussed the Marilyn Situation before, but we really couldn't understand why Arden put up with her crap when he never tolerated ours. Even though I knew how funny love was. I guess I only saw what I wanted to see. And it was so good to have Arden back. He was practically living at our house, The Drive, as he called it because of its location. Marilyn was always working or on the phone with the movie people, or investors (she was always trying to double her money), so Arden would come hang out with Stewart and I. We'd sit and drink coffee; sometimes we'd go out to lunch. It was casual, and Arden and I enjoyed it so much after the non-stop craziness of the last two years. During the week we'd hang out mostly at RPM's and listen to music; I was so glad that my music store felt like my living room. It was exactly what I had in mind when I designed it.

Sometimes we could convince Marilyn to join us for dinner, but those evenings were not as special to me. Marilyn had this way about her, something that hadn't been there before the movie deal. It was evident now that she thought everyone was beneath her. Nevermind that the rest of us had more manners in our snot than she did in her whole body. As my Daddy would have said, she was a piece of work.

It was Arden, who in the course of sly conversation convinced Stewart and I to tie the knot within a months time. I'd almost forgotten how good he was at that kind of thing. I surprised him back, though, by asking him to give me away. He assumed I would ask one of my brothers, but I felt it was a more appropriate job for Arden, and he was truly touched. Arden knew that I'd found the right man in Stewart, it was a sentiment that never had to be spoken.

So Arden and Sally and I started meeting at the shop almost everyday where we would brainstorm. I wanted to get married in my own yard, but they finally convinced me that parking would be a nightmare and so we agreed on my Godmother's house out at Big Lake. It was a beautiful setting on the water, surrounded by huge old oak trees. Aunt Betty, my Godmother, had offered the use of her house at the engagement party, so we ran with it. Aunt Betty was a very influential person in my life. There were abundant adventures with her while growing up, and she exposed us, my brothers and sisters and me, to everything she was into; especially music.

If we were with Aunt Betty, there was music. Is it any wonder I ended up owning a record store? And it made it all worthwhile that she loved the place and talked it up all the time.

As soon as the where was settled, Sally and I headed off to New Orleans to look for a dress. And to visit with Pierre and Joseph, and to buy baby things at Orient Expressed. Let's face it, if you're going to New Orleans, you should do it right. We found the dress at Pearl's Place in Metairie; a beautiful Vera Wang empire waist creation in ivory. I'd always wanted that cut of dress for my wedding day because I figured it would be the most comfortable while also being the most flattering, and I was right.

After we squared away the dress business, we headed over to Magazine Street to visit Pierre and Joseph. Pierre and Joseph have been my dear friends for years. Pierre is a highly respected New Orleans florist and Joseph is a hairstylist, also highly respected, and very recommended. They are as different as night and day. Literally. Pierre is white and gay, and Joseph is black and straight, with a beautiful fiancée, Natasha. Their shop is one of the most fun places in New Orleans and women fight to get in there.

"Darlings," cooed Pierre when we walked though the door. He immediately stood and held out his arms for both Sally and I.

"How are you love?" I inquired.

"Who cares how I am, look at the two of you. Sally, you are simply glowing with new life. And Nevers…well I don't know if I've ever seen you look this way. That Yankee must be making you very happy."

"That Yankee is going to marry our girl, Pierre," said Sally. Leave it Sally to deliver my news herself, selfish girl.

"You're lying!" came Joseph's shout from where he was working.

"No she's not," I said, "I finally agreed to become a bride. I figured at my age and all, this might be the last offer I get."

"Oh, Nevers, you are rotten. Fulla bullshit, as usual," said Pierre laughing.

"You are right Pierre, and that is why we love her," said Sally. She'd been getting all sentimental on me lately. I blamed it on raging hormones, but it was nice to know she felt that way.

"Amen," shouted Joseph in his best southern preacher voice.

Sally went to visit with Joseph then and Pierre and I sat down to talk flowers. He saw my vision of garden roses as being perfect. "Love it, Nevers," was his response. When Joseph finished with his client, he and Sally joined the discussion and the talk turned to Joseph's own impending nuptials, scheduled for early fall.

"Well, things aren't progressing as quickly as we'd like them to because Natasha had to return home to see her Grandmother who is very ill," explained Joseph.

"Oh, honey, I'm so sorry," said Sally, "You must give us an address for her in Germany so we can write and let her know we are thinking about her."

"Y'all are too sweet. That would just make her day," Joseph said.

"I been telling you for years these girls were raised right," said Pierre.

"And since y'all love us so much we can count on your help for this wedding, right? I mean we'll feed you and get you drunk, of course," I said sweetly.

"Of course," came the reply, in unison.

We made dinner plans with our boys and headed over to Orient Expressed. Now this store is known for their children's clothes, but let me tell you something; Orient Expressed has so much merchandise, you can get lost in there for what feels like days, long enjoyable days. I especially love the house wares, and jewelry. But this was Sally's part of the trip, really, so I shopped with her for shortalls and bubbles, onesies and blankets; nevermind that this baby wouldn't be able to wear most of this until he was six to eight months old!

We visited with our friend Lola, who ran the home sales department, and she recommended some things. Lola is a local New Orleans girl who knows everyone and everything, especially when it comes to being uptown.

"Y'all have just got to have this hooded frog towel for that baby, and I'll just ship it out to you after it's monogrammed," she said. Lola is all about a monogram.

We love Lola, or Lola from Nola, as Arden calls her. After making large purchases (and Sally yelling because I'd spent too much on her baby, my soon-to-be Godchild), we headed over to Parasol's for a Po-boy. I've just got to convince Stewart that we need a condo on St. Charles, or a little something in the Garden District. We had a great dinner with Pierre and Joseph that night at Joey K's. Sally wanted comfort food, and they have awesome spaghetti and burgers. We talked about the wedding, and finalized some plans; Pierre and Joseph would come out in the middle of the week to help get things ready for that Saturday. As usual, I hated to leave New Orleans. Even though it was only three hours away, sometimes it felt like another world, apart from everything, even the rest of Louisiana. When I got home that night I teased Stewart with small details of the dress.

"It has a very low scoop-neck front," I said, smiling slyly.

"Does that mean you'll put out on our wedding night?" he asked.

"You are bad, Mr. Wainwright."

"No, I just love you, future Mrs. Wainwright. And I don't care if all we do for the rest of our lives is sit on the front porch of this house; if I'm with you I'm all good."

"You lie. You know you'll have to be able to fish."

"Okay, you might be right about that, but you can come with me. You in a big straw hat, reading a book through your Jackie O shades…are you ready for bed yet?" he asked impatiently, reaching for my dangling legs.

"Bad, bad, bad," I scolded as I hopped off the kitchen counter and started running towards the bedroom.

The Wedding, The Cancer, and The Baby

The day of my wedding was glorious and sunny; a warm and inviting day, a day to be outdoors. Any girl who ever dreamed of having an outdoor wedding would have pictured the day I had. I would be lying, however, if I said I wasn't scared. Having my hair done and putting on my dress was fun, but the closer I got to walking down the aisle (or across the yard) the more terrified I became. And it didn't have to do with Stewart, I was ready to be married to him, I just began to think that maybe we should have done it in Vegas or something. We had talked about that, but because he had no family we wanted him to be surrounded by mine, because really, they were his family now.

But when Arden took my arm I knew I was going to be okay. He looked so dashing it was easy to believe that everyone was looking at him, not at me. And of course he made me laugh. That was the thing about Arden. His life with Marilyn was less than perfect at this point, but he was business as usual, calming my fears. I was grateful he was there for me, but it made me crazy that there was nothing I could do for him as far as his marriage was concerned.

"Sheldon Sinclair tripped over a display at Terra Cotta yesterday and knocked down hundreds in merchandise. It was fabulous," he said.

"You always know just what to say to a girl."

"Well, I know you're nervous. And Sheldon Sinclair is such an easy target, you know. Of course, tacky woman that she is, she just whipped out her gold Amex and told them to charge the damage. Never even apologized."

"Sounds just like her; hopefully my Mama didn't invite her. I'd just die if the cake table went flying."

"Or the booze table. Now that would be a tragedy."

And then Arden was laughing. By the time we got to the alter/podium, we were both cracking up. Arden kissed me on my cheek and handed me off to Stewart with a squeeze of the hand. Then he looked at Stewart and said, with that trademark Arden smile, "There is no replacement for this model, so you better treat her good or she might malfunction on you."

It was a beautiful ceremony; short, too the point and not overly cheesy. And of course a good time was had by all. There was dancing and drinking until the wee hours. I was glad that we'd sprung for Limousines to get everyone home. By the time Stewart and I got back to our house, we were exhausted. But when he was helping me out of my dress I relaxed, which led to quite a lovely wedding night. And the next day we left for our honeymoon. Lyle Gugino, the man Stewart sold the family business to had arranged a trip for us to the Virgin Islands.

I had always wanted to visit St. Croix, and it did not disappoint. We stayed at the wonderful Cotton House and simply indulged ourselves in doing nothing. I felt a little guilt, though, because it was just the two of us in a three bedroom, three bath house. My favorite part would have to have been the gallery out back with the grill, where Stewart cooked steaks, while I floated around in the pool. And the beach was divine, just off the back of the house, down a small set of steps. It is somewhere we plan to return with friends, so we can fill the house with laughter and more memories.

It was a couple of months after the honeymoon, when Sally's delivery was getting close, that I noticed the swelling in my abdomen. Having previously had a tummy tuck, I was unsure about the cause. It was too long past for there to be any kind of infection, but it made sex painful, and when Stewart started getting concerned I knew it was time to call the doctor. And we found out soon enough that it had nothing to do with my previous surgery; it was my ovaries.

Apparently some tumors, loaded with cancer cells, had taken up residence on my ovaries. I can't tell you how badly I took the news. The fact that they had to be removed was more than I could handle, and even though Stewart and my family and friends rallied around me, it is something, in the end, that a woman must come to terms with on her own. And I won't lie; it took some time for me. When my surgery rolled around, I thought I was ready. I had cried and mourned and yelled at God and figured it couldn't get any worse. Of course I should have known better. This is me we're talking about.

When I awoke from the anesthesia haze, Stewart was there at the bedside with the worst look on his face I'd ever seen, worse than when Lady LaRue died.

"What is it?" I asked, I could tell something was wrong.

"Let's wait for Dr. Paul, Nevers."

"No, you tell me right now what's going on, or I swear I'll sit up in this bed and strangle the life right out of you." I was scared to death, didn't he get that?

"Okay, but try to understand, this isn't something that could be avoided. It had to be done, Nevers, it was an absolute necessity."

"What the hell happened?"

"They had to take your uterus. Now, Nevers, stay calm, it's going to be okay," he said, trying to make me lie down and stay still. "Dr. Paul said he had no choice, that the cancer had spread. Oh, Nevers, I'm so sorry. But don't you see, you are going to be okay now. A couple of radiation treatments and things are going to be fine."

"A couple of radiation treatments? You mean they took my uterus and my ovaries, and I still have cancer in my body? Why didn't they just take it all? Why didn't they just rip every organ out of my body?"

I was getting hysterical at this point, I mean, who wouldn't? But Stewart stood there and listened to me cry and scream; he took my pummeling fists like they were hugs and kisses. By the time Dr. Paul came in, I was a little calmer and could really listen when he explained things. The cancer was gone, the radiation a precaution. And Stewart had passed a huge test. He had delivered the worst news I could hear and then he stuck around and helped me cope. I think he knew that it was better that I hear it from him and not the doctor. I needed to know that he had the strength in him to help me get through this, because it wasn't going to be easy.

And it wasn't. Aside from the physical limitations put upon me from the surgery, there was the emotional drama; the tears that would come from so far inside of me I thought I would drown. I never thought I was one of those women who *had* to have children, but having the option taken away was more than I could bear. And the radiation treatments were like lemon juice in a paper cut...let's just add insult to injury. It was a trying time to say the least. If I wouldn't have had Stewart, and my Mama, and my friends in my life, I don't know what I would have done. Sally, hugely pregnant, sitting by the side of the hospital bed crying with me. Arden in and out, trying to save his marriage (although we didn't know that then) and still making time for me. And Stewart and my Mama; my rocks. Stewart babied me and my Mama made me function.

"You need to get up and walk, Nevers," my Mama would say.

"But it hurts," I'd whine.

"And it will hurt worse if you don't move around and stretch those muscles," would come her reply. Just getting me out of the house and into the back yard was a major mission for her, and as usual she accomplished it.

The only other thing that bothered me, even though it was insanely small compared to the fact that I'd never have children, was the loss of hair. I hadn't had a lot to begin with, but what I did have was nice. I got lucky that it didn't all fall out, but how it fell out, well that was another story. I'd lose it from sporadic places; it was never an even process.

But my cousin, Eva and May's sister Nina Jane, came to my rescue. Nina Jane is a hairstylist and she knows how to find a good wig. I was amazed at how well it matched my hair color and at how well it stayed on. That was a big thing for me, having hair that stayed on. Now I could go The Kroger with no shame.

During this period of wretchedness, came baby Jackson. The one thing that I thought would really destroy me and push me over the edge, ended up being the one thing that could calm me and make me realize there was more than just loss in the world. Sally was an angel, bringing that baby over as often as she could; and I know it was a task for her to get out of the house with him. Stewart had even gone out on his own and purchased and then set up one of those porta-crib things for Jackson.

Those were good days, just sitting around and talking and holding that baby; even Stewart loved those days. Of course he'd almost been worse than Jack, waiting for that baby to arrive. It really is true that new life breathes new life into otherwise bleak situations. And when Arden was home we would all get together and Stewart would cook some dinner, or we'd order out and those, those were perfect times. I always thought of my problems as the storm, but I realize now that me and Sally and Arden coming together again was the calm…the storm was still brewing on the horizon.

The Detective

When I arrived on the scene, I didn't know what to make of the chaos. Having only moved to the Lake Charles area about six months ago, this was something new for me. I mean I'd been to crime scenes before, even ones with dead bodies, but this was just beyond belief. Wildlife and Fisheries had been called out to locate and tranquilize the alligator, and a big argument was going on as to whether or not they'd have to kill it to get body parts out...I mean really. And the body parts we found, well let's just say they were missing some features. My boss, Sheriff Arceneaux, was very interested in an arm that was pulled out. The wrist was all scratched up, like the deceased had been wearing a bracelet that someone had tried to pull off.

"These scratches are too small to have come from that gator, looks like maybe there was a struggle before she fell in," he said, chewing on the end of a really nasty looking cigar.

"Well, she didn't fall in Sheriff, that gator grabbed her by the foot and pulled her in. But the husband did say something about trying to pull her out of harms way, maybe that's where the scratches came from," I replied.

"Can't be sure, Owens. What if there was a struggle, now just what if, they were fightin' and he was trying to twist her arm and throw her in," Arceneaux mused.

"I'd say sir, that maybe you've been watching too much *Law & Order*. I mean, no disrespect sir, but did you see the husband when we got here? He looked like someone just rolled over him with a dump truck. The first deputies on the scene said he'd been crawling around in the dirt trying to find her, thinking he could still save her."

"He felt guilty 'bout what he'd done, Owens, felt guilty and couldn't take it back."

And this was the kind of small town mentality I was dealing with. I'd moved to Lake Charles to get away from the big city bullshit. Baton Rouge had gotten way too big over the last few years and I was tired of the senseless crime. Not that Lake Charles didn't have any, but usually it was different, and honestly, it just didn't occur everyday. I could have gone home to New Iberia, but I knew in my heart that wasn't the place for me either. My parents were both gone, and being an only child left me anchorless. I guess I could have gone a lot farther than I did, but I just couldn't bring myself to leave the south. So after my last long term relationship ended (because she couldn't stand the hours I worked, or the pay I got for those hours) I decided to go west, and I ended up stopping in Lake Charles, and I liked it, so I stayed.

Now here I was smack dab in the middle of this gator mess, with my boss breathing down my neck. "Figure out what's going on here, Owens. This is all too damn convenient," were his last words to me. So I did what any good detective would do, I went back to the office and Googled the deceased. Turns out she was a writer, just sold a screenplay and had been doing the Hollywood thing for awhile. Impressive. So I Googled the husband. Another writer, bestseller with his best friend (quite a looker, his friend). Hmmm.

It would make for a damn good plot, this death by alligator story. I started to think maybe my boss was on to something. I took all of this information to Sheriff Arceneaux and he ran with it. "Get all the financials, son. It's always about money with these artsy-fartsy types." I'm not kidding, he really said that. I wasn't sure that it was going to get me anywhere, but I called the DA's office and requested the damn things.

"Is this being investigated as a homicide?" asked Gert, the secretary for ADA Robert Whitman, "Because I've known Arden Mercer all his life and that would just be absurd."

"I really can't say, Miss Gert. Could you just please pass along the request? Thank you." And I hung up.

I could already tell that this thing was going to be a mess. Everybody in town knew Arden Mercer, and everyone in town was going to be up in arms over this. I myself didn't know him, but I thought it might be time to meet him. Maybe just talking to him could shed some light on the situation. It always helps to know who you're dealing with. After making a few phone calls, I found out he was staying with his writing partner Nevers Clark, so I decided to pay them a visit the next day.

Nevers and her husband Stewart lived on Shell Beach Drive, which I had been informed, was high class in Lake Charles. But their house was very unassuming, looking more like the houses I grew up around in New Iberia. It had the wrap around gallery and a gravel driveway, a porch swing rocked gently out front. And the landscaping was meticulous, yet lush, kind of like growing wild in an orderly way. The whole set-up was warm and inviting, not quite what I'd expected.

I went up the steps to the porch and knocked on the screen door. I took notice of the fact that there wasn't a doorbell and for some strange reason this also made me comfortable. When the door opened I was surprised to be greeted by a short, beautiful black girl. She must have noticed my stunned expression.

"Can I help you?" she asked impatiently.

"Hi. I'm Detective Owens from the Sheriff's Department. I was told I could find Arden Mercer at this address."

"Let me go get Nevers for you," she said, leaving me standing outside of the screen door. She acted like it was an everyday occurrence that I was there.

When Nevers came to the door I was surprised again. She didn't look like the same woman I'd seen in the picture. I mean, she didn't look bad, but she looked like she'd been through a lot, physically and mentally, since the picture was taken.

"Hi," she said, "Can I help you?"

"Yes Ma'am, I'm Detective Owens, Ezra Owens, from the Sheriff's Department. I was told I could find Arden Mercer here. If it's possible, I'd like to speak with him."

"Well, he's not doing all that great, but I guess you can come in and we'll ask him how he feels about it," she replied while pushing open the screen door. "Please, follow me. He's out in the den."

The den was a large room off the back of the house and one entire wall overlooking the back yard was glass, it was quite simply one of the best looking rooms I'd ever seen in my life. It had to be where they spent most of their time because the furnishings looked comfortable, but not worn. There wasn't anything ritzy, either, in this house. All the furnishings were very simple. And there were photographs everywhere, and I recognized the art of several locals adorning the walls.

"Arden, honey. This is Detective Owens from the Sheriff's Department. Do you feel up to talking?" She asked so sweetly; it was touching really. You could tell these two had been friends for a long time. I was just about to extend my hand to introduce myself when the black girl came back into the room followed by a tall, very handsome blond man wearing cut-off khaki shorts and an old t-shirt. He smelled of turpentine.

"Nevers, I'm headed back to the shop," said the pretty black girl, "You need anything later, you call me, okay?"

"I will. Thank you, Kiki." Then she took the hand of the tall man and introduced him. "Detective Owens, this is my husband Stewart, Stewart Wainwright."

"Nice to meet you sir," I said, shaking his hand. "And you too, Mr. Mercer. I'd like to ask you a few questions, if you're up to it."

"Sure, please, sit down," said Arden.

"Yes, please sit. Would you like something to drink? Some iced tea, or a coke? Nevers asked.

"If it's not too much trouble a glass of tea sounds wonderful."

"With lemon?"

"That would be great."

"Well, I'll butt out now," said Stewart, "Just wanted to see what was going on. Nevers will tell you it's the Yankee in me, always having to know what's cookin'. I'll be in the garage if you need me," then he kissed his wife and strode out the door.

I waited until Nevers came back with the tea before I asked anything of Arden. He looked so miserable I thought it best for him have someone in the room to whom he could turn to if needed. And I was right, because as soon as Nevers sat down he took her hand, and she smiled at him; a smile of utter confidence and belief.

"I know you've been through this already, Mr. Mercer, but I was hoping you could tell me again what happened.   You see, I've been put in charge of the investigation, and…"

"Investigation?   What investigation?   What is there to investigate? His wife was brutally attacked, and he couldn't do anything to save her.   What needs investigating?" She didn't understand where any of this was going and it scared the hell out of her.   She was worried and the protector came out in her.

"Calm down Carlotta," said Arden lazily, "She gets a little over protective at times.   Been that way since third grade."

"Well, if the damn papers would stop calling for a comment, it would be different. That's why I had Kiki here today. She works at my music store downtown; hell she practically runs the place lately. Anyway, she was here answering the phone," explained Nevers.

"Let it go, Nevers. We'd want the scoop, too, and you know it. Lake Charles is all about a scandal; that's why we love it. Look, Detective Owens, here's the story…"

And then Arden proceeded to tell me the story of how he and his wife had come to be at the Creole Nature Trail, and of the baby alligators, and even of her "damn shoes". He admitted to grabbing her by the wrist and yanking with all his might to try to save her, and yes, her diamond tennis bracelet did come off in his hand. Then he reached into the pocket of his slightly rumpled Citizens of Humanity jeans and pulled out said tennis bracelet. I wanted to ask for it, for evidence purposes, but I really didn't know if it was evidence of anything. This guy had been totally forthcoming, unnecessarily honest. I found myself captured by these two friends, their total devotion to one another.

After our exchange Nevers insisted that Arden lie down and rest, then she asked me to follow her into the kitchen. Just as we entered yet another beautiful room, the back door swung open to reveal a hopelessly cute woman carrying and equally cute baby. The woman had the face of a little girl, framed by a perfect bob. The baby sat right on her hip, and they looked like they had just walked into their own house, which of course they hadn't. This house was a haven for people, I decided. She was introduced as Sally, and the baby was Jackson.

"Detective Owens is here asking Arden some questions," explained Nevers.

"What kind of questions? Is he in need of counsel?" asked Sally.

"Not at this time," I replied. "But the investigation has been placed in my hands and I had not had the opportunity to speak with Mr. Mercer until today." I didn't know how my answer came off. If they really knew what the Sheriff thought they would be surprised to say the least. I thought it was best to be as vague as possible.

I decided to take my leave just as the baby started to fuss; these people had been through enough today. I could only hope I didn't bring them any more misery. When I got back to the office the financials were waiting on my desk. We were lucky in one aspect. Mrs. Marilyn Mercer had just transferred her accounts from a bank in New York to one in New Orleans, and there was an awful lot of activity since the transfer. It was also recorded that she had set up an off-shore account, and that was a piece of information that I found very interesting.

Things Start Getting Weird

"What the hell was all that about?" asked Sally.

"I'm not really sure. That guy really caught me off guard, and not because of his looks."

"You can say that again. Whew. Now, really, when was the last time you laid eyes on someone that good looking? All black hair and crystal clear blue eyes? Good, Lord."

"Are you done?" I asked.

"Lighten up Nevers. What did he want? Was he accusatory in anyway?"

"No, that's the weird thing. He just wanted to know what happened and I guess he wanted to hear it from Arden. I can only imagine what those deputies are telling him."

"And what did Arden say?"

"He told him what happened, just like he told us. The Detective did ask a question about her arm or something, like if she was wearing a bracelet, and Arden said yes, that it had come off in his hand while he was trying to pull her up. He even pulled it out of his pocket and showed it to the guy. I don't know if that was helpful or not. At least he didn't ask for the bracelet, that could have been bad."

"Well, I don't think we should worry too much about it right now," said Sally, "Let's take Jackson in to see his Uncle Arden."

But worry I did, it's in my nature. The next day when I went to the shop I worried, and it was draining. I really was feeling better physically, but my energy level was no where near what it used to be. And I was feeling pitiful because I just wanted things to be back the way they were. I wanted to go dancing with my friends; I wanted no cancer or bizarre accidental deaths in my life. I wanted some normalcy. And everyone around me saw it. Eva made an appearance at the shop that day and I could hear her and Kiki cutting up out front.

'What is going on out here?" I asked, using my I-know-you're-up-to-something voice.

"Nothing, Nevers, I swear. Kiki was just telling me about the good-looking man at your house yesterday. Think you could set me up?" asked Eva.

"Not with the man who is "Investigating" my best friend, no. I don't think so. Besides, what happened with Jacob? I thought y'all were all hot and heavy."

"You didn't tell her?" Kiki asked Eva, doing her silent laugh and pounding one foot on the floor. "That Jacob boy. He knocked-up some Chi Omega last year and decided it wasn't anybody's business. But Eva found out when that girl came beatin' on the door begging for diaper money."

"Eva, really?"

"Nevers, no one knew. And it wasn't the fact that he had a child, it was the fact that he hid it, and apparently wasn't taking care of it," said Eva.

"That boy is messed up," said Kiki. "I told you that the night you met him. 'Stay away from that,' I said, but you didn't listen, nobody ever listens to Kiki."

Which was a lie. We all listened to Kiki. The morsels of knowledge that sprung from her lips were too good not to hear. Kiki had been raised by her Grandmother in Jackson, Mississippi, and was fed one-liners all her life. And she was too smart for her own good. After her Mama died and she went to live with her Grandmother, the days of slacking were gone. She was expected to get good grades and succeed in life; which she did, graduating from Millsap's and going to work for an investment firm in Houston. But Kiki wasn't fond of the rat race, so she headed back to Jackson and started working retail and discovered that customer service was her forte. A few years later her Grandmother passed away, and Kiki found herself in need of something new. She had a friend in Lake Charles, someone she went to Millsap's with, who told her to come visit. Kiki arrived and to hear her tell it, "It felt like home."

I remember the day she came into the shop. She was looking for the new Common CD. We started talking about music and discovered we liked a lot of the same stuff, and she knew a great deal about the stuff she liked. When I found out she was a college grad and had just moved to town I offered her a job on the spot. And I've never regretted it. Kiki took the reigns when I got sick. It never occurred to her to bail on me; she just started running the show, which she is good at doing.

And she hired Wes, my other full-time employee. And Wes is another piece of work. At the ripe old age of 21, Wes had already seen more of the world than most people could ever dream of. He grew up an Army brat, and took in everything he could from every place he lived. Except Fort Polk. Wes couldn't grasp the good 'ole boy way of life, so with his parents blessing he headed off to Shreveport. But Shreveport didn't cut it for Wes either, he claimed that everyone was too stuffy, so he decided to try Lake Charles.

He liked the little downtown area, and he liked that the arts played a big role in the culture. For a kid who had never been settled anywhere before, it felt like home to him too. And the day he walked into RPM's and met Kiki, he felt like he'd found family. I remember the day that Kiki brought him to the house to meet me. I was still recovering from my surgery, sitting out in the back yard soaking up some sun. And here came Kiki with this tall, Nick Cave looking kid trailing behind her. I was immediately smitten in a motherly sort of way. We found him a great little apartment above one of the old banks, and he became part of all of us.

Sometimes I worry needlessly about the two of them in the shop together. Wes has a gift for memorizing movies, and he and Kiki will often only speak movie dialogue for an entire work day. It is something to behold. Or Wes will have his easel set up near the back of the store so he can paint when things are slow, and Kiki will stand there looking over his shoulder saying, "Why are you making that green?" And Wes will say in his most hippy tone, "Don't get in the way of the flowing vibes, man." Or, "You're messing with my chi, Daniel-son, go away."

The two of them side by side is a true study in physical differences. Kiki is only about 5'2" and has the most beautiful dark brown skin and green eyes (a gift, she says from her Great-Great Grandmother who had a fling with a white man), and Wes is about six foot, all lanky and wiry, and it doesn't help that he is into somewhat obscure music and dresses like a modern day Sid Vicious...tight t-shirts and tight jeans. Despite these physical differences, they are now brother and sister to each other. Kiki and Wes have brought all kinds of joy into my life. It is almost like God knew I needed them since I couldn't have my own kids. And they are the kids I would've prayed for had I been able to have my own. So I was glad to see Wes come in that day, when I was in worry mode. He had actually taken to calling me "Mama" and was always the first one to tell me not to sweat anything. "It'll all come together," was Wes' mantra.

"Whassup, y'all?" he asked in his best southern vernacular.

"Kiki was just filling me in on why Eva's last relationship failed," I explained.

"Cause he was a putz," said Wes, matter-of-factly.

"Y'all quit picking on me. And, Nevers, set me up with that cop who was at your house yesterday."

"Not the po-lice. Don't ever go out with a cop, Eva. That's asking for trouble," said Wes.

'He's not a cop, he's a Dee-tective," said Kiki, "And he could detect me anytime."

"Y'all are rotten," I said, "I've finished up my paper work, so I'm headed home. Open invitation for dinner tonight, I think Stewart is cooking fish. And it would be good for Arden to have company."

"We'll be there, Mama," said Wes as I walked out to the sound of the new Strokes album starting up.

It was almost sad, leaving them, even though Eva had a real job now. Believe it or not she had gone out and gotten her floral license and she was working at the best shop in town (now that mine was gone). I couldn't wait until I was feeling 100% and I could be at the shop all day. Sometimes I think that worried Kiki and Wes, but neither one of them was going anywhere. Even if the shop didn't make enough to pay them, *I* would. I was also glad that everyone was going to be coming for dinner, Arden needed that. I can't imagine what he's been going through, which is why I let him have all the valium he wants, but at some point he's gonna have to start thinking about things.

I was just getting into the car when my phone rang. I didn't recognize the number, so don't ask me why I answered it. It was Detective Owens. And all I could think was how the hell did he get this number. And then I remembered; he's a cop.

Excuse me, a Detective.

"Hi, Mrs. Wainwright, sorry to bother you but I had some information to pass along and I felt it would be better to talk to you rather than Mr. Mercer."

"What is it now, Detective?"

"Well, the Wildlife and Fisheries guys called a local guy to euthanize the alligator and the coroner will start the autopsy tomorrow. After that, they'll be ready to release the body. I didn't think that Mr. Mercer was up to making funeral arrangements, and, well, I just wasn't sure who else to call."

"You were right to call me. Have y'all been able to locate Marilyn's parents yet?"

"Her parents?" he asked, sounding confused.

"Yeah, you know, her Mama and Daddy?" I was getting a little tired of all this. If he was a detective, why had he not been detecting?

"Uh, Mrs. Wainwright, Marilyn Simone's parents died when she was ten. She grew up in a couple of different foster homes in New York."

"I'm afraid you looked up the wrong Marilyn then. Arden has been in the room with her when she's talked to them…Oh, wait, maybe they were her foster parents and she just never said."

"I'm not sure, Mrs. Wainwright, but I'll double check the social and let you know. And Mrs. Wainwright, I'd be very careful when you bring this up with Mr. Mercer."

"You don't have to tell me that. And, Detective, as long as I am going to be your go-between, you may as well start calling me Nevers."

"Sure, as long as you call me Ezra."

I sat there in the car thinking about the conversation. I just couldn't process what *Ezra* had been telling me. This was all getting stranger by the minute, and I was right in the middle of it. I had to get home and talk to Stewart before I lost my mind. And speaking of lost minds, when I looked up before pulling away from the curb, there were Kiki, Eva, and Wes, smashing their faces against the front window. I drove away laughing.

It was quiet when I got home. Arden was asleep on the couch in the den and Stewart was back in the bedroom, having just come out of the shower.

"There you are my gorgeous hunk of a husband. Give me one of those big shoulders to lean on." I leaned into him and stuck my head up under his chin.

"Don't tell me you over did it going to the shop, Nevers. You know you have to take it easy, doll."

"No, the shop was good. Eva stopped by and the kids made me laugh, and I got through all of my paperwork. It was the phone call I got leaving the shop."

"What phone call?"

"The one from Detective Ezra Owens. The phone call in which he told me that Marilyn had no parents. That her parents died when she was 10 and she was raised in foster homes. The phone call to let me know that what is left of her body should be ready to go to the funeral home in a couple of days. God, Stewart, it's just sick, all of it."

"Her parents are dead? Are they sure?"

"Ezra, as he asked me to call him, is going to double check her social again, but, you know, it almost makes sense to me."

"Oh, that's right, Arden never spoke with them. Isn't that the story?"

"Yep. He'd be in the room while she was on the phone, supposedly talking to them, but he never actually spoke with either one."

"Do you think you could get me her social? I need to make a phone call or two. Is Gavin's number in our book? They have to have some background information on her from when she was hired at Kelley Publishing, wouldn't you think?"

"God, I love you. My brain just isn't working. I knew though, if I came home to you with this, you would find some way to make it better," I said, wrapping my arms around his naked chest and planting a little kiss there.

"Whoo, now I've really got to get moving," he said with a grin.

It was only then that we turned around and saw a groggy Arden standing in the doorway. He looked like he was going to dissolve into tears, and then his eyes change just slightly and the look became full on anger.

"I knew it," he said, "I fucking knew it. You know, this doesn't surprise me. I never told y'all this before because I didn't want you to think that I was doubting my marriage, but this isn't the first time I found out she was lying."

"Arden, don't do this now. You're tired, and I want you to rest because everyone is coming for dinner tonight. I want us all to relax and just be together," I said.

"No, Nevers, this is the perfect time to do it. I didn't tell y'all this before because you woulda dragged me over to the mental hospital, but when it happened there was the briefest moment of clarity when I lost hold of her hand, that moment of shining light when all the stories you heard as a child came back. *Don't exact revenge on the people who hurt you, because they'll get theirs in the end.* Don't you remember being told that? Well, the clarity was that moment. It was like God looked down at me on that perfect day and said, here, let me take your troubles away. Y'all don't even know what shit I've put up with, even before I said "I do".

"That first trip to LA, she didn't have any meetings set up, she wanted to use my name to get in the door, and I was so taken with her that I let her. She bad mouthed you all the time, Nevers; said you didn't have any talent and that you didn't deserve any accolades, because I wrote most of the book. She took on Sally, laughed when Muffy died, and I mean fell apart thinking about the actual dynamics of it, and said that she needed some of the potion you used to get Stewart to marry you.

"But the worst thing she ever said was that she couldn't wait for my Mama to die because then we'd never have to come back to Lake Charles again. When I told her it wouldn't work that way because this was my home and I would always live here, she slapped me. And, Nevers, you know me. It took every ounce of decency in my body not to break her neck right there.

"I don't know why I didn't leave, so don't ask. Maybe it was because I knew from the very beginning that it was wrong, and I felt like a failure, maybe it was because she said if I ever left her she'd kill herself and make it look like I did it. And listen, I believed her. She was vicious. And here's the worst part...I hate that she went out the way she did, but I'm so glad she's gone. I think I've been eating the Valium for the last two days so I wouldn't bust out laughing. I mean ding-fucking-dong, the witch is dead."

And then Arden sat down on the side of the bed and started to sob; his whole body was shaking. I sat down next to him and put my arms around him and just held him. I felt so bad for him. It really is harder sometimes when you feel no guilt for something that should make you feel terrible. I looked up at Stewart, and he said, "Stay with him. I'm going to make some phone calls."

After about thirty minutes, Arden's breathing was calmer, and he'd stopped shaking. He looked at me aghast, and said, "Oh, Nevers, I am so sorry." I told him to shut-up. I made him get in the shower, and then I washed my own face and changed clothes. Stewart came in a few minutes after that and said he had news but we could wait until after dinner to discuss it, just the three of us.

"And I called Peking Gardens and ordered like one of everything, so I'm gonna go pick that up. Stay in here until Arden is out of the shower and then y'all get the table set. Jackson's crib is set up in the back bedroom and the monitor is all hooked up so we can hear him," said Stewart.

"Excuse me, but where is the phone booth you changed in?"

"I built one out in the garage."

Dinner Conversation

When Arden got out of the shower I made him come and set the table with me. It was probably a strange thing to do the day after your wife is mauled to death by an alligator, but it worked for us. Arden and I were both a little less emotional, and we were able to talk without falling apart.

"Do they think I pushed her?" he asked.

"I don't know, Arden, but it is strange that they would open an investigation into something that was clearly an accident. Was anything else going on that I should know about?"

"Not that I know of, but it's obvious that she lied about a lot of things, so who knows."

"Well, I would have to say that my biggest issue is with the phone calls. Who the hell was she talking to? And why even pretend that her parents were alive?"

"I've been thinking about that too. Maybe she was ashamed that she grew up in foster homes, but why? It happens to lots of kids, so what's the big deal?"

"I don't know, Arden, I really don't. But I will tell you this. I think it would be a good idea to have an attorney. And I think it should be a good old Southern attorney, not to trash my husband, but if anything should happen, I think you should have someone from here, who understands the politics, not some big shot from New York who will get lost in the semantics."

"I think you are right, Nevers, but who do we know? Most of the lawyers we've come in contact with don't deal in this kind of thing."

"I don't know, but I know someone who does. My friend M'Kay in New Orleans. She works as a stenographer, and I know she's seen a lot of action. I'm gonna go call her right now. Can you finish setting the table?"

"This is probably one of the only things I'm qualified to do right now."

I went back to the bedroom, found the cordless phone and dialed M'Kay's number. M'Kay and I had met a couple of years ago at *Look*, Pierre and Joseph's shop in New Orleans. We got to talking while we were under the dryers; actually we bonded over *Car Wash*, the old Rose Royce hit. It came on while we were sitting there and M'Kay started doing the claps at the beginning, and I started laughing. I think that the world as a whole sometimes forgets that music really does bring people together, as it did for M'Kay and me. I found that she was smart and savvy; she knew a lot about New Orleans, and politics, and the state of the city in general. She knew who was dirty, who was clean and who could be turned. Of course she didn't name names, but I knew that with this issue, she would give me honest answers, she'd let me know who the best person was to have on our side.

"Hello."
"Hey, M'Kay, it's Nevers. How are you?"
"Well, hey yourself. You know I was just thinking about you. The paper here picked up the story of your friend Arden and his wife. Tell me they were drunk? I mean, how else does something like that happen?"
"God, I wish I could tell you that. Look, it really was a tragic accident, but the Sheriff's Department has opened an investigation nonetheless, and I'm a little worried about Arden. He's holding it together now, but if they start to tighten the screws he'll lose his mind."
"I hear ya, girl. So what do you need?"
"Let me first say how nice it is to talk to someone and not have to pretend everything is okay.

We need a lawyer, a very good lawyer. The best New Orleans has to offer."

"Well, then. You need Mr. Trosclair, Mr. Jules Trosclair. He's the best, Nevers. He can argue the scales off a snake. He's what we call a refined old Cajun man. He's very smart, but he knows when to pull the "I'm just one of y'all" card. Let me get you his office number. His secretary's name is Beverly and she can be selective about scheduling appointments, but you just tell her I gave you his name and she'll fit you right in."

"Thank you so much, M'Kay. I'll keep you posted as to what's going on."

I hung up the phone and breathed a sigh of relief. If nothing else, we had good people on our side. I was still doubting that they'd bring charges against Arden, I mean really, what proof did they have. And if they really knew him they'd know that if he didn't kill Marilyn when she talked shit about his Mama, he never would.

I heard voices coming from the kitchen, then and knew I better get out there if I wanted a shot at holding my Godson before he was put down for the evening. But when I walked into the kitchen I knew I had missed my chance. Arden was holding Jackson out in front of him and talking away, and Jackson was just cooing and spitting bubbles the way all babies do…he was just infinitely cuter than any other baby in the world while doing it.

"Arden tells us he's lawyer-ing up," said Jack.

"We though it was best. I don't know how much Sally has told you, but we didn't think that it would hurt. If nothing comes of this whole thing, then great. But if they do decide to come after Arden, I want us to be prepared," I said.

"That's the way to play it, Nevers. It's already all over town that he was questioned, so people are going to start getting opinionated," said Sally.

"Well, piss on them," said Arden. "If they want to believe that, let them, but I'll tell you what…if I'd wanted to kill her, I'd have done it months ago. That's the thing; it was actually starting to get a little better. Maybe it finally hit her that I was never going to leave here and she decided to find something she liked about the place. Or maybe she found God and didn't tell me. I just don't care anymore."

"You know, I was somewhat of a Spin Doctor on the mayor's campaign a couple of years ago. That can be my job on this. And I need something to do; I need to feel like I'm helping" said Sally.

"Actually, you could write something up for the paper. Put all those pre-law courses to good use. I know they've already run with some info from the Sheriff's Department, but let's see what they're next move is before we go getting all defensive," I said.

"Sounds good to me," said Arden. "Once again, my girls come to my rescue."

"Yeah, they're good at that," agreed Jack.

Jack took Arden then and the two of them went to put Jackson down for a nap. Sally and I laughed listening to them over the baby monitor. Jack was explaining why it was beneficial to have Jackson sleep on his back and Arden, you could tell, was listening intently, while cooing soothing words to the sleepy baby.

Stewart came in a few minutes later and Kiki and Wes followed him through the back door. Within minutes everyone was greeting each other, hugging and laughing. Sure, we were avoiding to a certain extent, but it was easier to let the conversation come about on its own. No one wanted to be the one who started it. Sally took Kiki and Wes with her to peek at the baby, and I filled Stewart in on the whole lawyer thing. He also agreed that it was the right thing to do, and I could tell that he was proud of the way I'd handled it. But really, it still didn't feel like enough. Not after finding out what Arden's last year had been like. Part of me hoped they found Marilyn's head intact so I could slap her face.

Eventually we all sat down at the table and everyone filled their plates. Kiki told us a funny story from the shop, something about some kid wanting to know if we could order *Suburbia* for him on DVD. Kiki laughed because the kid was all of about nine years old. "I mean, I understand the boy needs some culture, so he could stop frontin', but c'mon." Apparently the kid is in love with Wes, and his mom works next door at the hair salon so he comes in all the time. We all laughed at Wes' mini admirer. And then came the lull. Praise God for shameless youth.

"So what's going on with all your stuff, Arden?" asked Wes.

"Wes!" I scolded.

"No, Nevers, it's okay. We're all family here; they have a right to know. And truth be told, I'd rather them hear it from me than read it in the paper." So Arden, who must have been much more clear-headed, told the story again.

"Damn man, that's just wrong," said Wes, stifling a grin. And it was contagious, because Kiki started laughing outright.

"I am sorry, Arden. Really. But this is some crazy shit. I know I've only been around for about a year, but I figured out that this kind of shit could only happen to y'all. I mean that. Like bad shit happens to all kind of people all the time, but y'all's ass gotta do it up different, you know what I mean?"

For a minute there we all just stared at Kiki, and then everyone at the table busted out laughing; including Arden. And I hate to admit it, but it felt good. Everything Kiki said was the truth, and at this point it was what we needed. It was bizarre, and scarier still, it was the kind of thing that Arden and I would write about. Our characters always met their demise in a most unconventional way. And as we all sat there laughing, no one heard Eva come in. As she made her way around the corner from the kitchen into the dining room Stewart was the first to see her. His eyes grew concerned and we knew that something was terribly wrong.

The Dropping of the Bomb

It got so quiet in the room that all you could hear was Jack Johnson's *Staple it Together* playing in the background. It was a soundtrack of your life moment, which pissed me off because I loved that song and now every time I hear it I'm going to think of the news we were about to get. Eva stood there for the longest time, looking right at me, and I could tell she wanted me to know what was going on without her having to say anything. She couldn't bring herself to look any where else. She was trying so hard not to break down. After a moment she walked over and took my hand. I knew something bad had happened that involved one of us, or Eva would have just blurted out what she knew. And that under the circumstances it had to be Arden.

"What is it, honey?" I asked.

"They're doing it," she said, "they are going to press charges. And then she started bawling.

"You are fucking kidding me," said Sally, never one to hold back. Arden just put his head in his hands. I don't think he was crying, I think he just felt like his head was going to explode and he was trying to hold it together.

"Well, we knew this was a possibility. Nevers, give me that lawyer's info. I don't care if it's late; we need to make contact with this guy," said Stewart.

"You're right," said Jack. "Let's get the ball in our court."

"Wait," said Arden, "how did you find out?"

"I was at OB's and I was talking to Ryan Guidry who works in the clerk's office. He said, 'Hey, don't you know Arden Mercer' and I said that I did, and he said, 'You know they are going to arrest him for killing his wife'. I started to argue, but his friend said it was true, that he'd seen the paperwork. And that's when I lost it. Richie had to drag me out of there and drive me over here. I'll be lucky if Ryan doesn't press charges."

"Why? What did you do?" asked Stewart, falling into father mode.

"Well, I threw my drink in his face and then pulled him off of his barstool...and, well, I started kicking him," she explained.

"What shoes are you wearing?" asked Sally. Eva raised up one foot to reveal a very cute pair of Lulu Guinness pumps, with a very pointed toe.

"Shazam," said Wes, speaking for us all.

I pushed my chair back and got up slowly. My physical and mental were merging together at this point, and I felt the seriousness of the whole situation sinking into my bones. I said a little prayer at that point; *God, I need to be of use to my friend. Grant me the ability to withstand whatever else may come our way. Let me be strong for those who need me.* Stewart took my hand and he and Jack came with me to the bedroom to get the information I'd written down earlier. Then the two of them holed up in the living room at the computer desk and got to work.

I headed back into the dining room where Kiki and Wes were clearing the table. I gave Wes a kiss on the cheek and said, "Thank you." He looked at me like I was nuts. Sally had gone to check on Jackson, who had started to stir. It was just like a baby to feel the tension from three rooms away. Arden was still sitting in his chair and Eva had gone to stand behind him, her arms draped around his neck. Arden was holding her hands tightly, like he was trying to gain strength through her. If it wasn't such a delicate moment, I would have gone to grab my camera. The two of them were a study in raw emotion and it was beautiful in its own way. Sad, but hopeful.

"Arden, honey, do you need to go lie down?" I asked.

"No. Really, I'm okay. I was expecting this Nevers. I think what I need is a pen and some paper so I can start writing everything down. I need to get it all out, and then this Trosclair guy, if he takes me on, will know everything."

"I think that's a good idea. Let me grab you some stuff. And I'll make some coffee."

"What's going on?" asked Sally. She'd just come back into the room as I was walking out.

"Arden wants to write some stuff down, get his thoughts together before meeting Mr. Trosclair," I explained.

"Good idea. I'm going to get my cell out of the car and call Gert from Whitman's office. I want to know what the hell is going on."

"Will she tell you?" I asked.

"Hell, yes. She and my Mama go way back. A couple of years ago her son got sick, I don't remember what it was, but it was bad. Anyway, my Mama and her prayer group started praying for him and he recovered just weeks after that. Gert always thought it was the prayer that brought him around. It was probably a good run of antibiotics, but who am I to argue? She'll let me in on the particulars, at least."

"Well, it's better to know something rather than nothing," I said, "Get moving." I grabbed Arden a legal pad and a pen and went back to dining room. He sat for a minute staring at it.

"I'm not sure where to start," he said.

"Start at the very beginning," I said, "back when we very first met her. That first meeting with Kelley Publishing. Trosclair is going to need as much background as we can give him."

"You're right. Nevers," he said tentatively, "what if it all goes bad?"

"Arden, it isn't going to go bad. You have too many people on your side. She has no one. And I know that sounds bad, but if they want to make a case against you it will be hard without any witnesses for the prosecution. I mean, Kelley Publishing can say she was a good employee, but that's about it. And even that won't hold much water because she left them high and dry when she sold her screenplay. I feel really guilty talking shit about someone who can't defend herself, but that's just the way it is. And honestly, I care more about your well-being than anything else at this point. By the way, have you spoken to your Mama?"

"I did. I told her not to worry about the funeral; at that point that's all we thought was going on. She's supposed to be gone another three weeks and really, I don't think being here for a trial would do her any good. I'll just tell her they're investigating and leave it at that. Maybe there won't even be a trial."

Arden's Mama had been in France since the day before the accident. She was on a pilgrimage to Lourdes with her church group; even though she told us before she left it was really more about a cheap trip to France than anything else. I hated that she was out of the loop, but Arden was right, she would worry incessantly and that wasn't good for her health. Let her be in France, and whatever gossip reached her there, and trust me it would; well, we could say it was blown out of proportion traveling across the Atlantic.

I left him alone to write figuring that my presence wouldn't allow him the concentration he needed, and I went to find the kids. Eva, Kiki, and Wes were in the kitchen. Wes was finishing up the dishes, and Eva was silently sobbing while Kiki held her, saying, "Girl, it's gonna be alright. From what I hear, this lawyer is off the chain. He's gonna hook Arden up, you hear me?" Well, Eva heard her, and of course laughed, which was the outcome Kiki was trying to achieve. I fussed at Wes, telling him he could leave the dishes, but he wouldn't hear any of it.

"You shouldn't be doing all you're doing now, Mama. You think I'm gonna let you stand here and wash the dishes, woman? I think not. It's inconceivable," he said, waiting for the standard reply.

"You keep using that word. I do not think it means what you think it means," I said, taking the bait.

"This place is a nuthouse," said Eva.

"Yeah, well, maybe that's why it feels like home," said Kiki laughing.

"Bliggety-Bow," said Wes, which meant, I wholeheartedly agree.

I walked the kids out after that and found Sally sitting in her car talking on the phone. I got in on the passenger side and listened for a few minutes until Sally wrapped up the call.

"This shit is unbelievable," she said. "Un-fucking believable."

"What's going on?"

"It has to do with financial shit, but I don't understand how. Arden has more money that Marilyn ever did, so if someone was gonna get killed over money, wouldn't it have been him?"

"That would make more sense. Do they have anything else?" Not that the money wasn't something, but it is a motive that I've never understood. Furthermore we all thought Marilyn had her own.

"I don't think so and what they do have they are keeping under wraps. I think that means it's weak, don't you?"

"Yeah, but that doesn't mean it won't fly. Let's go let the boys know what's going on," I suggested.

When we got back in the house Jack was in the kitchen on the phone. He held up a finger for us to wait where we were. I scooched up onto the counter and Sally took a seat at the breakfast table, which is a really stupid name for a table, because we ate all kinds of stuff there all the time. I could hear faint laughter from the dining room and I knew that it was Stewart and Arden. I couldn't imagine what they were laughing about, and it sounded so good, I didn't care.

Jack got off the phone within a few moments and we all herded back into the dining room. I could feel my energy fading; it was pushing 11 o'clock and I had done way more today than I normally do. I tried to be positive though; thinking that I'd sleep really well tonight and wake up ready to go tomorrow. Apparently I was gonna need it.

"Okay," said Jack, "my friend who works for the Sheriff's Department said they are supposed to pick Arden up tomorrow. Now Sally, Nevers, don't y'all go freaking out."

"Look, we talked to Trosclair and he's going to leave New Orleans as early as possible, he has to tie up some loose ends at the office. They can't question Arden until he gets here. And he is coming," explained Stewart. "He is being paid very well to be at our beck and call until this whole thing is over."

'Sally, tell them what you found out from Gert," I said.

"Well, she said it has to do with finances, but she didn't have the particulars. Does that make any sense to you Arden?"

"Not at all. I paid for everything. I mean she did her travel stuff for tax purposes, but other than that, it all came from me," he said.

"Can you check your accounts online?" asked Stewart.

"I think I can access most of it."

"Let me get you my laptop," I said.

I fetched the laptop and we set it up on the dining room table. Arden found the website and immediately had access to his checking and savings accounts. Then he ran into a problem. His password that logged him onto his investment accounts was denied.

"Are you sure you entered it correctly?" asked Stewart. "Try it again to be sure," he urged.

"I'll do it again, but I know I entered it right. It's my Mama's maiden name, and, well," he was stammering and then we saw the look on his face change. "That whore was the only other person who knew it. She wanted to switch banks and I was showing her how my investment portfolio worked. God in heaven, she was swindling me," he said with a look of amazement on his face. "That trashy whore was stealing my money. What has my life turned into? Should we call the *Days of our Lives* people and sell them this shitty story?"

"No, no, no. Look, we all need some rest. Now that we know what's going on, we know where to pick up the thread tomorrow," said Jack.

"Arden does anyone else have access to that account?" I asked.

"Well Jackson does."

"What do you mean, Jackson does?" asked Sally.

"I mean, if anything should happen to me, it all goes to Jackson. He is my godchild."

"Is that just in case of death or does incapacitation count?" asked Stewart. "Because if it doesn't, Sally needs to be named on the account."

"I'm gonna call them right now and leave a message on the voicemail. I'm gonna tell them that Sally and Nevers have permission to access my account, and if they give y'all any shit I'm gonna pull all that money out of there as soon as I get out of the joint."

No one could help it. We all started cracking up.

Carrie Comes Back

It had been so long that it really caught me by surprise. But I was exhausted and vulnerable. After everyone left that night, and I finally got around to it, it didn't take long for me to fall asleep. I'd gone to the master bath not so much to wash my face, as to throw cold water on it. I wasn't trying to wake up, but my head felt cloudy. There was just too much going on. Stewart was still cleaning up and I was trying to make it to bed before he came in, because he'd lecture me about not getting enough rest. Which is funny because after my surgery he and my Mama couldn't get me moving fast enough. Now it was all about resting. Which I guess makes sense because it was really the chemo that did me in. Either way, I didn't want to hear it, not tonight.

I pulled on my favorite Vicky's Secret cotton jammies, camisole top and elastic waist cropped bottoms. I was immediately comfortable. I made my way into the bedroom and crawled into the bed. I don't know if the sheets had ever been so soft and cool; it felt that good to lie down. It wasn't that there was pain, I just felt like I couldn't take another step. The big down pillows supported me enough to see the television, so I turned it on, hoping to get lost in something mundane and fall asleep. But of course there was a *House* on USA that I didn't get to see last week and I got all wrapped up in it. By the time Stewart did come in I was immersed and started shushing him when he tried to talk to me. "Fine, I'll leave you alone," he said with a smile and went to get in the shower. Stewart knew that I was a television junkie. Maybe it was all the time spent in front of it in my youth. All I know is that sometimes, especially when I get hooked on a show, you can write me off. I'm worthless. And *House* did this to me. I think it was a combination of the medical and the humorous.

Probably the most aggravating thing for Stewart is that being the reader that I am, if I'm into a book and a TV show I'll read during commercials. He knew all this before he married me, though. Before the nuptials he sat through many a battle between *ER* and a new Dean Koontz novel. He really is such a good guy. When I think about all the times he's put up with me and my friends I wonder why he's stuck around. He says he finds it amusing, but sometimes I wonder if the day will come when it bores him. He says no. He came in after his shower smelling clean and looking incredible. He's started to fill out a little since moving here, and it looks good on him. Of course I always think he looks good, especially in his boxers and a t-shirt, which happened to be what he had on.

"So what's going on?" he asked in reference to the television.

"This woman is sick and tried to kill her baby. They're trying to figure out what's wrong with her."

"Oh, cool, what's-his-name is walking. They left us hanging on the last one we watched." He was referring to the Omar Epps character who we liked. See, I turned him into a television junkie, and he likes it.

"Yeah, but he's too happy. He's driving House crazy."

"That sounds about right."

We lay there for awhile longer, sucked in by the story. So much for watching something to put me to sleep; I was wide awake. When it was over, I turned off the idiot box, as my Daddy used to call it, and said goodnight. And then I laid there in the darkness trying to find sleep. It wasn't long before I felt Stewart's hand on my hip, and then his breath on my neck. I turned around to receive his kisses. As tired as I was, the invitation was welcome and I think he knew that. I can't sleep when I worry, and something about sex releases all my tension. Kind of like a massage, but you don't feel like you have the flu for the next two days. When all was said and done, I was putty. There was nothing else I could do *but* sleep. Until about 2 a.m. That's when I woke up with a start, screaming and terrified, having had the worst dream of my life.

Carrie. I didn't see her in the dream. But she was there. In the dream I was sitting in front of her plaque, you know those tacky things they've started using instead of headstones? Anyway, I'm holding an armload of gorgeous yellow roses, thorns and all. They are scratching up my arms. And there are more on the ground all around me in a circle. The trees are closer to me in the dream than they really are at the cemetery, and oddly enough, there are no other graves around. It is very quiet and very still. Like she wants me to concentrate, so that's exactly what I do. I'm staring at nothing, past what I can see. And then I hear it. Marshall Tucker Band, *Can't You See*. But I'm still looking too far out to see what Carrie wants me to see. I'm listening to the music and becoming totally absorbed.

And then the songs starts to wind down and tears are quietly streaming down my face. I reach out my hand to touch the plaque with her name on it and through the tears I can see a name, but it's not Carrie's. The plaque says: Arden Mercer. And that's when I woke up screaming. Scared to death. My poor husband didn't know what was going on, but he knew enough to get a hold of me and calm me down. Now, Stewart has seen me talk in my sleep, I mean carry on conversations, he's seen me cry in my sleep, but, he'd never witnessed this.

"Baby? Nevers? Its okay, baby. Whatever it is, it's okay," he was repeatedly whispering close to my ear.

"Oh my God, Stewart. It was his name on the plaque. Arden's name. He was dead. Oh, God." I couldn't catch my breath, I was freaking out.

"Be still, Nevers, it really is okay. I've got you. Just tell me what's going on." So I did. And then he was a little freaked out.

"I don't think we should tell any one about this, okay? I mean I just think it would cause a stir," he said.

"You're right. This would freak Arden out. It's not the kind of thing he should hear right now," I agreed.

"I'm still kind of confused about the whole thing, though. Carrie dreams are usually pretty forward. You've always known what she was trying to say."

"I know. And they've never been scary, but this one...Well, this one takes the cake." I hit me then just how incredible my husband is. I don't think that any one else in the world could be so supportive of a wife who has dreams about her dead best friend. The fact that the Carrie dreams are always indicative of something notwithstanding, most people would have thought I was out of my mind.

"Come here," Stewart said, pulling me close. I knew that his sweetness would make me start to cry again, but I didn't care. I let the tears come.

The Shyster

I can assure you I was not happy when Beverly called me at ten o'clock on a Sunday night to tell me some people in Lake Charles needed my assistance. "They're friends with M'Kay," she said. Like that made a difference. But it did, it made all the difference in the world. It is because of M'Kay that I am in the position I'm in today.

About ten years ago when I opened my own practice M'Kay saved my ass. It was during a trial that wasn't going so well. I had questioned my client, the accused, and then passed him off to the prosecutor. What we didn't realize was that he'd incriminated himself. I was nervous as all hell and didn't catch it. So when he denied it during cross, the prosecutor asked to have it read back. And M'Kay, for some reason had transposed the whole sentence. God Bless her. It was just luck, I guess. She later said she was just having a bad day.

But that mistake made a big difference in my life. People who didn't believe in me before then thought I had connections, which couldn't have been farther from the truth. M'Kay didn't even know what she'd done until I told her. The judge was too old and senile to weigh in on the issue, saying he heard it the way M'Kay read it back, but that was just to cover his own ass. It was a comedy of errors that changed my life. For the better.

I was a kid who grew up in Grand Isle, Louisiana. What did I know about the legal system, you may ask? For a long time, nothing. But life is a teacher. And then my stepbrother, who was about 20 years older than me, went to Vietnam. And what they thought a little Cajun boy was gonna know about fightin' a war is beyond me, but he was a good shot, so they wanted him. He served as a sniper for more time than he should have and he came home broken. After that it was one arrest after another. He ended up killing a guy in a bar fight in New Orleans.

And he was represented by a public defender. My brother felt so much shame, he couldn't look at our Mama or at me, and when they convicted him he left the courtroom without a word. Three days later he hung himself. That's when I went to the library and started reading up on the legal system. I knew if my brother had had a good lawyer none of this would have happened. And it was then that I promised myself I was going to be that good lawyer. I worked my way through college and law school and went to work for a firm in New Orleans. But that firm didn't want to give me a chance, I still had that accent, they'd say. You'll get laughed out of court for that alone.

So I learned everything I could from them and then took off on my own, scared to death. And I was still scared the day M'Kay saved my ass. Now she had a friend she wanted me to help. It wasn't as if this had never happened before, but in most cases it was something that could be handled over the phone. Never had it involved murder. And after a few phone calls to Lake Charles I learned that this is how they were classifying it. I didn't see it that way.

The accused, one Mr. Arden Mercer, was a pharmacist at one point in his life. The way I figured it, if he'd wanted to kill his wife, there were much easier ways. Pushing her into the open jaws of an alligator was risky. What if she wasn't killed, but simply mauled? There were too many questions. And what was the motive? The Sheriff's Department said it had something to do with finances, but Mr. Mercer's friends, who filled me in on all that was going on, never once mentioned money; even after I quoted them my fees. It just seemed like it wasn't an issue.

So now I was on I-10, heading west. I'd passed Baton Rouge and was traveling through Cajun Country, as they call it, wondering what waited for me in Lake Charles. Beverly had dug up some information for me, which I glanced at before I left. Arden Mercer was an author, made the best-seller list with his best friend Nevers Clark Wainwright. Married to one Stewart Wainwright. Now that name I knew. The Wainwright family had been around for ages, and at one point owned a couple of publications in New Orleans, but that was probably way before the current Wainwright could read.

So, Mr. Mercer had influential friends. Did that mean he thought he could murder his wife and get away with it? Probably not. Actually the whole thing felt wrong. I was eager to meet the characters in this drama. Sometimes people don't understand that just laying your eyes on someone can give you all the answers you need. I also found it strange that the Cameron Parish Sheriff's Department had passed this mess on to Calcasieu Parish. What did the city of Lake Charles have to gain from this? As far as I could tell, nothing. It wasn't an election year, which meant that the Sheriff wasn't trying to drum up votes, and he had Ezra Owens working the case, and Ezra Owens was good. I met Owens years ago while working a case in Baton Rouge, and he could have become my nemesis.

But Owens understood the dynamics of Louisiana law; he understood that the regular folks that live off the land here did not want to be hauled into jury duty and then be told what they should think. Which is what the prosecutor in that case did. Which is funny to me because those "regular" people know more about life than a half-wit politician ever will.

So, yeah, I was interested in getting down to Lake Charles and figuring out just what the hell was going on. I was interested in meeting my client and his friends. And I was very interested in finding out why Owens was in Lake Charles, and just what his whole take on the situation was.

The Meet and Greet

The next morning found me up first, although I wasn't alone. I'd convinced Sally to leave Jackson because he'd had his last bottle of the night and was sleeping so soundly. I couldn't believe that he'd slept through the scream last night; he and Arden both. But he was such a good baby; even when he awoke this morning, it was not with cries, but utterly adorable baby speak. I made him his bottle and we were sitting in the big chair in the den when Arden came in. He leaned over and kissed Jackson and then me on the top of our heads.

"My worst fear is coming true, Nevers."

"I know. They're taking you to a place were the sheets are a poly-blend," I said with a straight face.

"Not only that. I am something to behold in the looks department, and that has me a little worried."

"Just play hard to get," I advised.

"Okay. I'm going to have a nice long hot shower because who knows when I'll have the chance again," he said, and then added, "Alone," a little melodramatically.

"Communal showers. Just like high school."

"God, don't remind me," he said.

Arden and I had talked last night after everyone left. During that time we decided to start acting like Nevers and Arden again. That meant no more feeling sorry for ourselves. Sure we were scared, but we'd always used humor in frightening situations. This situation would be no different and the humor was very needed. We knew, however, to watch what we said in mixed company. It wouldn't do Arden any good to be cracking jokes in front of law enforcement. But it felt good this morning, especially after the dream that I couldn't tell him about. And the talk the night before had been good for us too.

Arden told me so many things he had promised himself he'd never speak of.

The time he spent with Marilyn changed him in certain ways. Of course the biggest being a lack of trust when it came to dealing with anyone outside of our immediate circle. And he knew that that would change over time, as would his feelings about women. He was scared to death of any kind of a relationship at this point, which was understandable, and I told him so.

"Maybe I'll act like it's the 80's again and just sleep around," was his solution.

"You'll be in demand when all this is all over. Girls love a bad boy," I said. "Oh, maybe we could do a jailbird wedding, you know over the phone or something tacky like that."

And so the joking started. And it felt good; like when Kiki made the comment about this whole situation being right up our alley. I knew that even if we didn't laugh now we'd laugh later, so it just made sense to start when it was most needed. As I sat there, holding my Godchild in my arms, seeing him smile at me while holding the bottle tightly between his gums, I felt a peace I hadn't felt in a while. I took it as a good sign because I knew that our lives could change in an instant. Stewart came in a few minutes later and took the baby from me.

"I love the way he smells in the morning," he said.

"I do too. Kinda like sweet dreams." He knew what I meant. After last night I could use some sweet dreams. I also told him about the conversation that took place while he was on the phone last night with Lyle Gugino. I'd forgotten to tell him before bed because we were so involved with the TV, and then…anyway, I told him what Arden and I had decided and he grinned the good grin, the one that always made me want to kiss him, so I did.

"I'm glad Nevers. Things were so serious last night. And I know we have big issues to deal with; starting yesterday, but I also know that you and Arden and Sally have so much support to give each other. And I know what form it usually comes in."

"I knew you'd understand. Keep smelling that baby, Arden will fight you for him when he gets out of the shower. I'll go make coffee. Sally should be here before too long and my Mama is coming to watch the baby while we get done all the things that need to be done."

"Where's Miss Rose?" he asked, in reference to Sally's Mama.

"She's in France with Arden's Mama. Praying for us all."

"Good, we're gonna need it."

I made coffee and then headed back to the bedroom to get dressed. We weren't sure what time they were coming to get Aden so we wanted to make sure we were ready. Mr. Trosclair had left a message earlier that he was just past Jennings and would be here shortly. Stewart had given him directions to the house. By the time I finished getting dressed, my Mama and Sally had both shown up. Stewart said my Mama had stolen the baby from him and we laughed because there she was walking around the kitchen holding that baby like a dishrag on her hip and doing a million other things.

Arden came out a few minutes later and went straight for my Mama, giving her a hug. "Hey, Kay," he said in his good boy sweet voice. Arden was the only friend I ever had who got away with leaving the "Miss" off when addressing my Mama. Mama poured us all some coffee and we were settling in at the dining room table with the paper when we heard a car in the driveway. "It's a big truck," said my Mama. And then we all went to the window to look, like it was some kind of anomaly that a lawyer would drive a big truck. Stewart, coffee in hand, went to answer the door. We listened as Stewart introduced himself and you could hear Mr. Trosclair's presence through his voice when he responded. A deep, strong voice, not unlike that of my Daddy, but Trosclair's was tinged with that Cajun drawl. I just knew that when he was tired he'd say "dat" instead of "that".

When they came into the dining room I think everyone was surprised. For some reason we had pictured him as older; a regal gray-haired distinguished looking man. He was distinguished looking, but I would put him mid to late forties, which didn't jive with the picture I had in my mind. He was a good-looking man with caramel-colored skin that was as smooth as Jackson's butt. And he had beautiful hazel eyes. His hair wasn't quite high and tight, but it was neatly trimmed, keeping what looked like black curls under control. He wore jeans and a suit coat over a beautiful black cashmere sweater, and loafers that looked Gucci in origin. He was about 5'10" and stout, but he carried himself well. He reeked of money in a good way.

"I apologize for my appearance, but I didn't want to drive in a suit," he said, like he wasn't presentable.

"Oh, please," I said, "we are all very casual around here. Please come in and meet everyone. I'm Nevers, this is Sally LaFleur, and this is my Mama, Kay Clark. And this is your new client, Arden Mercer."

"Arden. Glad to finally put a face with the name," said Trosclair. And without missing a beat he gave Arden the most casual once-over I'd ever seen. But there was also something in his eyes, like he could tell if someone was guilty just by looking at them. He was good though. I don't know if anyone else saw it happen.

"Nice to meet you, Mr. Trosclair," said Arden. "Thank you so much for coming all this way at such short notice."

"Well, I won't tell you this case didn't interest me. But even more interesting is your assembled group here. They raised quite a stink for you. Not often a man has this many good friends at his side."

"They've been this way since about third grade," said my Mama. "We used to question it, but it never did any good, as you can see. Didn't matter what kind of trouble it was, they were always backing each other up. Now y'all sit down, I'll get the coffee." We did as we were told. Mama poured coffee for everyone while we brought Trosclair up to date on the finance thing.

"Sally and I are going down to the bank this morning to learn what we can about the password being changed and to see if we can't get statements," I said.

"That would be most appreciated, as I assume I will be in court with Mr. Mercer all day, and since this is all preliminary I don't have anyone with me to do the normal legwork required. And if Mr. Mercer will sign this power–of–attorney then you won't have any problem accessing the account. Do you have any objections to that, Mr. Mercer?" asked Trosclair.

"Not at all. The people you see at this table are the only people I trust anymore, yourself included," said Arden.

"Good, but I have to ask, just how did y'all find out about the finance aspect of it?" Trosclair asked.

"It's all small town networking," explained Sally. "My Mama prayed for this lady's son a while back when he was ill and the lady happens to be the Assistant District Attorney's secretary. I don't want her to get in trouble though, and really she didn't tell us anything, just that there was a 'finance issue'."

"Don't worry about it. Arden and I can play dumb until the charges are brought. They will have to supply a motive, and if that's what they're basing the motive on, well then that just makes us one step ahead."

"I like the way you think," said Stewart, which made everyone laugh.

After some more small talk, Mr. Trosclair went out to his truck to get his suit and then I showed him to the back bedroom where he could freshen up and change. "Beautiful home, Mrs. Wainwright,' he said. "Thank you; we've put a lot of work into it. And please, call me Nevers. I have the feeling we are going to be seeing a lot of each other." We both laughed after that and I decided then that I really liked Mr. Trosclair. I knew, after studying him a little, that he was going to do a good job. He was a listener; and even when the conversation was all over the place this morning, he still managed to hang on.

The morning had been so nice. It is strange, I know, because we were waiting around for the cops to come and arrest our best friend. So when the doorbell rang later, it was like someone dropped a crystal stem at a dinner party. It shocked us all. I mean, we knew what was going to happen, but comfort got the best of us. Stewart answered the door and invited Detective Owens in like we were having guests for brunch. Following Owens was another deputy, this one scrawny and malicious looking.

He was introduced as Deputy Dupree. I took one look at him and knew that this was gonna be the guy who put the cuffs on Arden; in fact he looked like he was itching to do it the minute he walked through the door. I despised him immediately. And I reveled in his disappointment when it was decided that Arden wouldn't be cuffed at all. I wanted to trip him on his way out the door. Detective Owens had decided that handcuffs were not necessary, and I wondered about that until I heard Trosclair call Owens Ezra.

"Just so y'all don't think this whole thing is tainted," explained Trosclair, "Detective Owens and I go back quite a ways. I met him years ago working on a case in Baton Rouge, and in my opinion he's a good Detective."

"Did you win that case in Baton Rouge?" asked Arden.

"Yes, I did," said Trosclair.

"That's all the information I need," said Arden. "Let's get this over with."

I could tell that Arden was starting to get very nervous, and I couldn't blame him. If it was me, I would have been crying like a baby. But he held it together, and before being led out the front door he said, "Make sure the towels are warm from the dryer tonight. I don't want to catch a chill getting out of the tub." I had to restrain myself or laughter would have erupted and we would have been in for it.

Arden walked out with Detective Owens, and Stewart and Trosclair followed. Owens put Arden in the back of the Sheriff's car and closed the door. It was a horrible sound, and I couldn't help but start crying. "Get in this house right now, Nevers. It won't do Arden any good to see you fall apart," said my Mama, and she was right. Stewart and Mr. Trosclair followed Arden to the courthouse in Stewart's Jeep. Arden needed someone there with him, besides his lawyer, and Stewart volunteered. He always said if it wasn't for Arden he wouldn't have won me over, and it's probably true. Arden gave him a lot of insider information that helped. Stewart always knew when I was about to get antsy, and calmed me before it happened; because of Arden he knew that it was just the way I operated. Arden took all my game away.

With the boys off to the courthouse, I dried my eyes and blew my nose and Sally and I got ready to head over to the bank. My Mama was perfectly content with Jackson, although when he went down for a nap I knew she'd either re-pot my plants or get on the computer to play solitaire. Just knowing that she was gonna be there when we got back made me feel better, though. She's always been my rock. When my hair was no longer patchy and Nina Jane was able to create a style from what I had left, my Mama was the first one to say how well it showed off my features; instead of mentioning how gaunt I looked. Technically it was a man's haircut, but I was loving the ease of it, but I still kept a wig around for when I wanted to look glamorous.

Gathering Evidence

Sally and I headed over to the bank. As we drove Sally explained that she understood my breakdown when they took Arden away, but that now it was time to get angry and get things done.

"But I can't be mad without being mad at myself," I said.

"Why would you be mad at yourself? You didn't do anything wrong."

"That's not true. We are both a little to blame. We should have known that there were problems worth mentioning. Maybe had we said something, they never would have stayed together and this shit wouldn't have happened. I just keep thinking there had to be something we could have done."

"God, Nevers, you really know how to pour it on. Let go of all that shit, please. This is not our fault, and it isn't Arden's either. Marilyn was a bitch. Get that through your head. I don't know if it's because she grew up without parents and in foster homes, if that's even the real story, or if it's just because she was some kind of control freak. But her selfish personality got us into this. Had she not had to get close to those alligator babies, had she not worn those goddamned shoes…It was her, Nevers. Lose the guilt."

"I know you're right, but it is so unfair. And I want to help him so bad. It's killing him that his Mama is not here, too, but I understand why he won't tell her what's going on. I just want to *do* something for him."

"Then put on your big girl panties and let's get in that bank and find out what's going on."

The bank was eerily quiet when we walked in. I figured a Monday morning would be busy, but I guess people were still trying to figure out where their money had gone over the weekend. We were shown almost immediately to Elliot Reyes office, one of those partitioned cubicles that banks are so fond of. Like it matters if there's a half wall. People can still hear what you're talking about.

"What can I help you ladies with this morning?" Reyes asked.

"We need statements covering every transaction made on this account," I said, putting the power-of-attorney right under his nose, and mentally tugging on my big girl panties. Sally gave me a smile. Reyes studied the POA and then asked to see our ID's. We whipped those out staying one step ahead of this guy. He was staring to look pale, and I was starting to get suspicious.

"One moment, please while I make copies of all this," he said, rising from his chair and sagging out of the cubicle.

"Something is going on here," said Sally softly.

"No shit," I whispered back. "You think his hand was in the cookie jar?"

"I don't know about the cookie jar, but I'm almost positive it was somewhere it shouldn't have been." As Sally said this, Reyes walked back into the office, looking sheepish.

"Everything looks in order. Let me just pull up the account and see what we have," he said.

About a minute later the printer was spilling out paper, getting us one step closer to what was going on. Sally snatched them out of his hands and started looking over them.

"These are all actual banking transactions, money moving. We also need to see records of authorized users, password changes, that kind of thing," she explained.

"Um, I'm not sure what you mean," said Reyes.

"Look, we need to know the name of every person authorized access to this account, and we need to know when they accessed it. Basically, this information that you've printed out, but detailed as to who did what and when they did it," I said. If Reyes had been looking pale before, now he looked like he was on the verge of vomiting. And the weird part was that he had to know why we were here, yet he hadn't asked. He did some more typing and the printer started up again. Sally grabbed the new pages out of his hand.

"Is this all of it?" she asked.

"Yes, Ma'am."

"Oh, and we'll need copies of the original paperwork from when Mr. Mercer opened this account," I added.

"Sure, let me get that for you." And he was gone again.

"Don't you think it's strange that he never even asked us why we were here?" asked Sally.

"I was just thinking the same thing myself," I said.

When we got everything we asked for we headed out into the sunshine, leaving the shady bank and its shady employees behind. It was still a little early for lunch, but we pulled through the Tony's drive through and ordered a Tony's Special. We sat in the parking lot looking at the stack of papers in our possession. We'd already decided to wait until we got back to the house to go over them, so the seats of Sally's car felt like they were made of pins and needles.

"So, why do you think a Tony's Special is so special?" she asked.

"Because of the tiny the ground meat," I said.

"And why does their root beer taste better than everyone else's?"

"It's the perfect mix of ice and root beer, and the fact that it comes in the styrofoam Tony's cup. There's magic in that cup," I said laughing. And Sally laughed too, and for some strange reason we felt a little better.

We got back to the house and Mama was just putting Jackson down for a nap, which worked out well for us. We told her about how things transpired at the bank and she said, "I see." Leave it to my Mama, but those two words really did sum it all up. I mean, whatever was going on, and there was something, would have been discovered at some point, even if Marilyn had not bit the dust. So Sally and I spread out the papers on the dining room table and while we crammed Tony's pizza down our throats we started to read. My Mama shared some pizza with us and then headed for home. So it was shocking, an hour later when the phone rang. Sally and I had been so immersed in the bank statements that we'd lost all track of time. I ran to find the phone before it woke up Jackson.

"Hey, honey," said Stewart.

"Hey, what's going on?"

"I just wanted to call and let you know we're on our way home."

"Who's on their way home?"

"Me and Trosclair....And Arden."

"You're kidding?" The feeling of relief was beyond fabulous.

"Nope. This Trosclair guy is good. He got Arden released without bail, pending trial. Trosclair told the judge that since Arden's finances were part of the investigation it would be best if they didn't have to be accessed. And really, I think that the judge knows the charges are bullshit. Look, I'm pulling up in the driveway. See you in a sec."

And within a minute they were in the house. Sally and I ran over and hugged Arden who looked beat; then I threw my arms around Trosclair in a moment of pure emotional abandon. Thank God he laughed. Had he pushed me away, I don't know what I would have done. When the three guys smelled the remnants of our lunch, however, they got a little irritable, so I called Tony's and ordered a bunch of po-boys and a family spaghetti. Then I got in the car and cranked up George Michael's *Freedom*, singing way too loud all the way back to Tony's.

After eating, Trosclair explained what was going on. Sally and I had a sneaking suspicion as to what it was, but we let Trosclair lay it out. First, Marilyn moved all her accounts to a bank in New Orleans, she didn't want the account here in Lake Charles, but she wanted it close. Then she started funneling money out of Arden's account to hers in New Orleans; that way if she was found out she could say she was just transferring to cover her expenses. She'd let the money sit for maybe a week and then she'd transfer it to an off-shore account in the Cayman Islands. "She really was trying to be high class, wasn't she," said Arden. All in all she made off with about 2.5 million of Arden's dollars, and he was not happy about it. But the thing is, he didn't know anything about it until today. Of course the Sheriff's Department thinks he knew about it for a while and was just waiting for an opportunity to take revenge. That's when we all laughed, because if Arden had known he would have left her immediately. He had already taken so much crap from her; the money business would have been the last straw.

"Let me explain how this is going to work," said Trosclair. "They are going to start interviewing people, and that includes all of you. And you are going to want to do your best to cover for Arden, that's only natural, but don't do it. Be honest at all times or something you say could come back to bite us on the ass. Even if it sounds bad, tell the truth. I'm going to drive back to New Orleans today to settle some things and get my stuff. What you have to remember is that this could be over tomorrow, or it could take months. It's all in how we play our hand."

"The trial starts in two weeks, right?" asked Sally.

"Yes. Unless they decide to offer us a deal. But we won't be taking any deals, so I will be prepping for a trial," said Trosclair.

"I heard someone say something about tourist from Arizona being there that day. Do you think they have a witness?" asked Stewart.

"I'll be going through their list tonight, but I don't think I'll find any surprises. Of course there could have been people there, but that doesn't mean they saw anything."

"There was another car in the parking lot, but I don't know what the plate said, I don't know much of anything anymore," said Arden.

"And what about the money? Does he get that back?" I asked.

"It has been moved into a separate account and is being held as evidence. When Arden comes out of this clean, it will revert back to him," explained Trosclair. No one asked what would happen if Arden didn't come out of this clean.

The Detective

I have to say, I was glad to see Trosclair on the case. I had been doing my job and following orders, but to me; well I just don't think Arden Mercer pushed his wife. So I was glad when it came time to start interviewing people. Glad to get out of the office, and happy about talking to people whom I assumed would be positive when it came to Mercer. I wasn't able to get in touch with his Mother, but that was okay because that would have been biased testimony anyway.

My first stop should have been the Wainwright house, but Arden was there, so I didn't want to go that route. And I really thought I should talk to people who knew him in a professional aspect, so I started with his former employees, people he worked with, that kind of thing. You see, there are people you see on a daily basis that you just don't think about all that often. The guy at the convenience store who listens to your cell phone conversation while you make yourself a fountain drink, for instance. You are familiar with him, you always say "Good morning." But do you ever think about what he hears during his work day? Your co-workers are the same way. I tried to explain this to my ex one time, but she didn't get it.

"He was a great employee," said Mr. Klein, from the pharmacy where Arden used to work. "The older customers loved him because he always had a moment to chat, or answer their questions. We weren't happy about it when he left, or the way he left, but look what happened. He got famous. We don't hold anything against him, and these charges are ridiculous. Even if what people are saying is true, he'd have never dealt with it by killing that wife of his. He's smarter than that."

I also talked to some of Arden's co-workers, I talked to a guy who had remodeled his kitchen, I even talked to one of his teachers from high school, and I always got the same thing. Arden was a dying breed, a nice guy. I liked to think of myself the same way, but I wondered what people would really say. I decided to talk to an old girlfriend, next. Maybe she would shatter the mold. I went to her house which was located in Barbe Court, not far from Arden's own. It was a nice brick ranch affair, unassuming, but nice. Sharon Darbonne was now married with a baby on the way, but I could see where Arden found her attractive. She had long brown hair and very green eyes all set against the backdrop of very bronze skin. She said that she'd just returned from vacation, which explained her color.

"Oh, Arden," she said, "I can't believe he's been charged with killing his wife. It's nonsense. Everyone knows it." I was starting to see a trend in these interviews. No one I had talked to so far had used the word "murder". I was beginning to wonder about it, so I asked Sharon.

"That's vile. It's appalling enough that they are saying anything at all, but to use that word, well it's just bad manners. There's a difference between killing and murdering. Murder involves something ugly, like drugs or sex; it's something that happens in New Orleans or Houston. And it's not something that Arden is capable of anyway."

She went on to tell me that she and Arden had fun while they dated, but that dating Arden was dating Nevers and Sally too, and that it started to get old. "We weren't serious, or anything, so when it was over it was okay. I mean, I really liked him, but I was ready to settle down, have that wedding and then some babies, and I don't think he was there yet. He is just the sweetest guy, though; and he understands women, he really does. His Mama brought him up right." This was unbelievable to me as a detective. I was beginning to think that there had to be another side to Arden; an evil side that no one ever saw. How could any one be so nice? I decided to head to the only spot I could think of for getting a different opinion. I mean, if the ex-girlfriend didn't have anything bad to say, where else could I go but a bar.

So my next stop was OB's. OB's has been around forever and still had people on staff from Arden's college days. It was someplace where he obviously felt comfortable, and I figured, if he felt comfortable there, he might have said things, especially while drinking, that could be used against him. I waited until Happy Hour was in full swing before I started asking questions.

"Yeah, I know Arden. Why?" asked Richie, defensively. Richie is the head bartender, and he's been around forever.

"Look, I'm just talking to people, trying to get a feel for the guy," I explained.

"I'm sorry, but no one here is all that happy about what's going on. Arden is a good guy, you know, a nice guy," Richie said sincerely.

"What do you mean, a good guy, give me some examples."

"Let's put it this way. I've known him for about 15 years and I only saw him lose his temper once, and that was back when they were in college." I took "they" to mean Arden, Nevers and Sally. There weren't too many stories that didn't involve all three of them.

"What happened?" I asked, not knowing what to expect from a well-mannered guy like Arden.

"They were all in here one night, just hanging out, you know this place used to be a lot cooler then, not the hip place it tries to be now. Anyway, some frat boy starts hitting on Nevers and ends up grabbing her boob. Sorry, her breast. So Arden has some words with him. And the guy says, "Who are you? Her boyfriend?" And Arden says, "No, her best friend. And you need to keep your hands off her." And then the guy threw a punch, but Arden, you know, he might not look like it, but he's strong. I've worked out with him at the Y before, I know. But, okay, so the guy throws a punch, which Arden catches, and before you can blink, Arden takes the guy out with one punch to the nose. It was beautiful."

"Did the guy press charges?" I asked; if he had it was something there would be a record of, an actual blemish on the pages of Arden's perfect life.

"Are you kidding? The whole bar saw what happened, the boob grabbing and the punches being thrown. He knew he'd get blamed," Richie summed up.

I talked to a few more people while I was at OB's and it was pretty much the same story. No one had ever seen him lose his temper, and even when he got really drunk, no one ever remembered him doing anything that would be called into question. He was everyone's favorite guy. I had decided to call it a night, so I ordered an Abita Amber and sat down at the bar. The boss was not going to like what I had to tell him in the morning, but unless he had someone else for me to talk to, this was all he was gonna get.

And, I'll admit, it was a little depressing. I didn't really have too many friends, and the ones I had were nowhere near the state of Louisiana, and often wondered why I was. What kind of legacy would I leave if I died tomorrow? They'd say I was a good cop, but they always say that when someone in law enforcement dies, even if they were dirty. And I'd never been all that lucky in love, and I really wanted to be. Actually, what I wanted was what Arden and his friends have. I wanted to come home from work, not to an empty house, but to a wife, and a baby; maybe a dog. Anything but the television and a bag of take-out. It was always so quiet when I got home that it kind of freaked me out.

But this was wrong, to be sitting here thinking about all this, bringing myself down wasn't going to help the situation. And that was when I noticed the brunette across the bar. She looked familiar, but with everyone I'd talked to today, I had to confess, I couldn't place her. And looking at her I thought there was no way she could have been someone I'd talked to, because she was beautiful, and I wouldn't have forgotten her. She looked upset, though, or maybe pissed off. I wasn't sure. Some women are just hard to read, and this girl, well, I definitely wanted to know her story. So I sent her a drink to see what the reaction would be.

Richie served it, pointing to me at the same time. There was no change in her facial expression, but she did get up and start to walk in my direction. I watched her coming around the bar, getting stopped once, where she smiled at someone, and then she was walking again. Where had I seen that smile before? This was driving me crazy. Normally I was very good about remembering details. And then she walked up to the bar and said something to the guy sitting next to me, who then got off his bar stool and walked away. Then she spun the stool around and looked right at me and I'll be goddamned if I didn't get that little flutter in my stomach. Dumb ass.

"You must be Detective Owens," she said with a slight drawl.

"And you know this how?" I asked.

"What, you think people aren't talking about you being in here? This town is small, despite the population. If you haven't figured that out yet, you might want to look into another line of work." God, I was loving this girl. She was a smart ass without being a bitch; a great combination in my book.

"Well, I have been making the rounds, but that's part of my job. Have we met before?"

"No we haven't. I'm Eva," she said, and then there was a pause before she added, "Nevers is my cousin." That was the smile. But it ended there. Different faces, different coloring, different bodies, but the same smile.

"It's nice to meet you, Eva. Please, call me Ezra."

"Really? You are investigating one of my close friends for killing his wife (there it was again, I thought), shouldn't it be 'Detective'? She was being coy now, testing me.

"I'm not investigating him now," I said. "Right now I'm having a beer with a beautiful girl, and I have to say, enjoying myself immensely." And I finally got the smile. And as she sat there, I realized I was headed for trouble, but I didn't give a shit.

We ended up sitting at the bar, drinking and talking until about eleven. When the nighttime crowd started to take over we decided to go to my house, even though we'd had too much to drink to make that decision. I insisted that she ride with me and she didn't put up too much of a fight. When we got to the house I grabbed us a couple more beers from the ice box and we settled in on the couch. We'd been talking about what it was like to live in Lake Charles, and I discovered it wasn't too different from New Iberia. Small towns are the same everywhere, everybody knows everything.

To be honest, the whole time she was talking, I was listening, but I was also thinking about kissing her. I knew it wasn't the alcohol, either. Because I wasn't quite drunk enough to do it. She was right, I was investigating her friend. Sitting at the bar in public was one thing; sitting on the couch in my darkened living room was a totally different matter, and really I couldn't figure out what she was doing here. That's when I started to get paranoid, and I think she knew, because that's when she kissed me. And as they say, that's all she wrote. The rest was a blur, which I hated because I wanted to remember everything. Of course there was always next time.

But when I woke up the next morning, late, and she wasn't there, I wondered if there would be a next time. I hoped there would be, but picking up a girl at a bar and sleeping with her that night was not something I had experience in. I'm not saying I'm old fashioned, but I almost always met the women I dated through mutual friends. So when I went to bars there was never the temptation. Oh, okay, there is always temptation, but it's not something I ever acted on. Especially when the woman was involved, even slightly, with an investigation I was working on.

It was eating at me, the whole situation, when I drove to work that morning. If it did get out, I was in trouble. I hadn't been in Lake Charles long enough to be part of the "Good Ole Boy" network. Of course I could lie and just say I gave her a ride home. That was close to the truth. As long as I didn't say whose home I took her to.

I was also worried that Eva would think I was some kind of player, that maybe I was trying to get information out of her. But that couldn't have been farther from the truth.

I could not look at that girl and think a single coherent thought at the same time. I had to find a way to apologize to her without making it sound like what happened was a bad thing. Because I thought, no matter what else was involved, it was one of the best things to happen to me in a really long time.

Nevers

The next morning found me sitting in the big chair in the den, feeling the effects from the night before...

It started with a bottle of wine after the house cleared out. Me, Stewart and Arden, sitting around the dining room table, each trying to figure out what to do next. Stewart had put some of the best people he knew for this kind of thing on the hunt for information on Marilyn's parents. Her birth parents had died when she was 10, that much we knew was true.

"So who the hell was she talking to on the phone?" wondered Arden.

"I have these guys looking into her foster care situation. If it was one of those families we'll find out," said Stewart.

"She was hiding something," I mused. "Why else would she not tell Arden? None of this makes any sense. What have we heard from Kelley Publishing?"

"She didn't have to list any information about anyone other than herself, so nothing."

"Did Trosclair say anything else before he left?" asked Arden.

"Just to rest. Even though we have two weeks to trial, he's prepping for all the investigating and he said he's bringing back two assistants, and we may have to help with them. You know steering them in the right direction, literally, because they won't know their way around," I said.

"What I wouldn't give to go to The Kroger," sighed Arden.

"We could put you in one of my wigs," I suggested with a stifled laugh. Arden didn't think it was too funny.

"I don't think I'd look too good in a page-boy."

"We could take you to The Super Wal-Mart; no one would know you there."

"Bullshit. When have you ever been to the Super Wally World and not run into someone you know? It's a high school reunion just waiting to happen."

"Here's my question. Why doesn't The Wal-Mart sell music with explicit lyrics, but they'll sell movies that have all the same stuff?" I asked. It really was something that bothered me, although I couldn't tell you why.

"Who knows why they do anything at that place. You know, they'll never be Target," said Arden.

"Absolutely. And let me tell you, I will buy Isaac Mizrahi over Kathy Lee Gifford any day. There's no competition there. I just wish Target had fabric. Fabric is the only reason I go to The Wal-Mart. Imagine; fabric from Target. Now that would be something."

"All that would mean is that upon leaving Target you would have a receipt in your hand for $200 instead of $100," said Stewart, and Arden laughed out loud, which was so good to hear.

"I gotta say, Stewart, you really do know her."

"The information you passed on in the beginning was priceless, Arden. It helps keep her in line."

"Y'all better quit picking on me," I said. "We have more important things going on."

"Yes, Nevers. But here's the deal: I don't want to talk about those things. They suck. And here I thought being a recluse would be fun. I'm sick of it, and it's only been like four days," said Arden.

"Maybe you can come to the shop with me tomorrow. That'll get you out of the house. And if you don't want to talk to someone you can hide in the office."

"Well I guess being a recluse in two locations is a little glamorous. It would be better though if you had some tinted windows on your car, and an awning out in front of the store. That would be a perfect photo op."

"The accused seeks shelter from best friend and local business owner," said Stewart.

"Oh, my God, I love that," laughed Arden. "Do you really think I'll attract some paparazzi? I mean there isn't too much else about this whole situation that's fun, you know?"

"Who knows? Maybe we'll start planning strategic sightings. And you know that the shop is a great place to get the inside scoop on what people are saying. We could start a "Free Arden" campaign," I said.

"Except he's not locked up, so it would have to be a "Drop the Charges" campaign," Stewart pointed out.

"Either way, it could be fun," said Arden. "Much more fun than thinking about the alternative."

I was thinking of that conversation while sitting in the big chair drinking my second cup of coffee the next morning. I knew there had to be something I could do to lift Arden's spirits. And a plan started to come together in my head, something totally outrageous that would have to be kept under wraps for the time being. I figured I'd run it past Stewart and Sally, but that was it. No one else could be privy to this plan.

When Arden and I got to the shop later, we walked right in the front door. No big Jackie O sunglasses, no avoiding the paparazzi, mainly because there were none. And it did feel good to be out of the house. The shop always brought out something good in me. Owning a record store was something I'd always wanted to do, and

I was proud of it. It was comfortable and spacious, and over the last year had taken on more personality from Kiki and Wes, than I could have ever given it on my own. The eclectic taste of the three of us made it an interesting place to be. The walls were now covered in movie and music posters; from *The Usual Suspects* to *Gone With the Wind*, to the more recent *Hustle and Flow*, and *Walk the Line*. And then there were the concert posters I'd found on e-bay for the *Sex Pistols*, *Cake*, and *The Beastie Boys*; not to mention the local ones for guys like Marc Broussard, and *Cowboy Mouth*.

It was a fun place to be, which is why I had decided to get Arden out this morning. Sitting in my house watching daytime television would have done nothing to lift his spirits, unless he's like me in the fact that watching some of those shows does make me feel better about myself. I mean really, even on Dr. Phil. Sometimes I just want to reach out and slap the TV. When we got inside I heard that Wes had put on some John Lee Hooker and was going to town dusting while Kiki was sweeping. I figured they must have wanted to get out early the night before and left the cleaning for this morning. With them, I really didn't mind.

"Well, look what the cat dragged in," said Kiki.

"We had to get out of the house," I explained.

"Yes, the paparazzi were beating down the door," said Arden, lowering his sunglasses and peering over the top of them.

"Man, no kidding?" asked Wes. This was really the first crazy thing he'd been through with us, whereas Kiki was becoming an old pro.

"Yes, kidding. There were no paparazzi. Arden thought it would be fun to be a bi-location recluse, and I live to indulge him."

"Well, kick back," said Kiki. "Wes and I will be finished in a few minutes and we can all shoot the shit. We tried to get out of here early last night to meet Eva at OB's, but a shipment came late, and by the time we got there she was gone."

"Rumor has it she was hanging out with that Detective guy," said Wes, with one hand on his hip and the other swishing away with the feather duster. "Richie said he was there talking to people about Arden. What is up with that?"

"I'm guessing they are trying to find someone who'll say something bad about him. But they'll be hard pressed to dig anyone up around here," I said.

"Yeah, there's plenty of dirt on me, but none that's even remotely criminal," Arden agreed.

"I'm sure Eva gave him and earful anyways. She's pretty damn good at telling people where they can get off," Kiki said with a laugh. By now, more than a year later, everyone in town knew the story about Eva telling off one of my customers at the flower shop. The woman was a bitch anyway, so I never cared, and it didn't hurt business.

"I'm going to make a few phone calls," I said, excusing myself. "Y'all behave while I'm gone."

I went back to the little office and closed the door which was not something I usually do. My first call was to Stewart who was on the road, headed to Home Depot to get more stain for the boat. Sometimes I felt bad because I had the shop to give me something to do, but Stewart said not to worry about him. He'd been working in the family business since high school and welcomed the break. He reminded me all the time that that is why he sold it. He didn't want anything to do. I quickly told him my plan. Thank God he thought it was a good one.

"Only you could come up with this, Nevers. It's brilliant, but it will be tricky. It shouldn't make headlines, if you know what I mean."

"Yeah, I know, and I have an idea about how to pull it off, but it involves Sally, and to a lesser extent, Jack and Grant." Grant being my brother-in-law who owned a beat up truck that was perfect for the mission.

"Then have at it, babe. I'm right behind you."
Good Lord, I love that man. Sometimes it seemed like the crazier the plan the more he loved me. My next call was to Sally who didn't even think of what could happen, she just laughed and laughed.

"I don't even want to know how you cooked this one up," she said.

"I really was just thinking about ways to cheer Arden up, and I thought, 'What if'. I mean really, if we can pull this off, Sally…Well it would be better than *The Italian Job*. Do you think Jack can find the guy?"

"Oh, yeah. He knows everybody down there. Let me call him so he can start looking into it. Where are you so I can call you back?"

"We're at the shop. I thought it would be good to get Arden out of the house, and this is a safe place."

"Okay, I'll do one better. I'll bring Darrell's for lunch. Are Kiki and Wes there too?"

"Yes. And go all out, please. I'll foot the bill."
To which Sally said, "Shut-up!"

I called Grant after that and he said anytime I needed it the truck was mine. Didn't even ask what I needed it for, just, "You know where the keys are, Nevers." Sometimes it's good to be me. And this plan gave me all sorts of renewed energy. I hadn't felt this good physically in months and this was after tying on a little one the night before. Maybe it's true that you do have to

get up and get moving to feel better, but I hated to admit that out loud because then my Mama would be saying, "I told you so!" A few minutes later, however, laughter from the front of the store brought me out.

"What's going on out here?" I asked.

"Eva's forehead," said Kiki.

"Look AT it," said Arden laughing hysterically.

"It is pretty bad," chimed in Wes. So I turned to look at Eva, who had walked in only moments before, and there in the center of her forehead was a huge round bruise, just starting to turn a scary purplish-blue color.

"What in the hell did you do?" I asked.

"Nothing," she said. "I mean I was drunk and ran into the bathroom door, it's not a big deal." But the more I looked at it, the more I could tell it didn't come from a door, it was too circular in nature. I knew that bruise.

"You are lying. That bruise is not from the door," I said, smiling. "That bruise is from a headboard!"

"And how would you know that?" asked Kiki.

"Well, y'all always wondered why we only have pictures from the first couple of days of our honeymoon," I said.

"Too much information. La, la, la, la, la, la," sang Wes, so he could block out the conversation.

"Here's my question," said Arden, "if that is a bruise from a headboard, just whose headboard was it?" And that was when Wes lost it.

"Not the cop?" he shouted. "They said at OB's that you were hanging out with that Detective. Say it ain't so," sang Wes. But Eva just stood there, looking guilty.

"It's not like I meant for it to happen," she said, defiantly. "He sent a drink across the bar; I mean it's not like he knew who I was. But I knew who he was and I knew he'd been asking questions so I went over there to put my two cents in. I just don't know how the rest happened."

"I know," said Kiki, "That man is hot. Like off the chain hot, he wouldn't have to do much to get some girl up in the bed with him."

"Good, God. It wasn't like that. We had too much to drink, and we both should have known better. That's why I got out of there before he even got up this morning. And that's why I'm here. I need someone to take me to OB's to get my car."

"It's only like three blocks," I said.

"But I don't want to be seen walking to get my car. Could someone please take me?"

"I will," said Kiki. And it was a good thing that they left when they did because customers had started to trickle in. I took Arden back to the office with me and Wes handled the front.

"Are you gonna kill her?" I asked with a smile.

"God, no. Maybe she won us points or tainted the whole investigation. Either way, it really doesn't have anything to do with me," he said.

"Well she'll be glad to know that. She's feeling the guilt; I can tell."

"Besides, I haven't laughed like that in days. A fucking headboard bruise. Leave it to you to figure that one out."

"The guilty always recognize, you should know that."

"Except I'm not guilty. At least not of this whole Marilyn thing. There's plenty of other things I'm guilty of, though." We had a good laugh at that one.

The Plan Takes Shape

Sally came in later with Darrell's po-boys for everyone, and sweet little Jackson in his car seat. We told her the story of Eva while we were eating and she cursed us because she was laughing so hard she almost choked. It was pretty funny, and I'm glad that Arden wasn't upset with her. I've said it before; if you live in Lake Charles you only know what's here. I'm sure that part of the reason Eva was so smitten with Detective Owens was because he wasn't from here. It didn't matter that he was still from Louisiana, he was different; he wasn't a local. And he is pretty damn good-looking.

There had been a couple of people in and out of the store all day, but no one paid much attention to the fact that Arden was there, which was good. It felt like a regular day. The girls from the hair salon next door came in and bought a couple of CD's which they then asked Wes to help them upload onto one of their laptops so they could put them on their iPods. It was just another service we offered for those who were not all that technologically advanced. Wes complied with a smile, wretched flirt that he is. "Right this way, Ladies. Let me show you how it's done." When Arden and Kiki started talking old R&B, Sally and I headed back to the office to follow-up on the conversation we'd had earlier.

"Okay, Jack found the guy. Wildlife and Fisheries got called out before the cops could make a decision, so the Sheriff's Department found some old local guy to do the job. Apparently it wasn't his first time, because he gutted it with the crime scene guys standing on the side of the road waiting for their catch. Sorry about the pun." Of course I laughed. Which was probably not nice.

"So he still has it?" I asked.

"Well no one really wanted to buy the meat, so he's holding out for a good bid on the hide. And the way I see it, no one around here could top our bid," she said.

"Yeah, but we have to be discreet. If we walk in there and offer him ten grand everybody from the Holly Beach to Shreveport will hear about it."

"I thought about that. So I had Jack ask around about this guy. Apparently he would like to buy a new boat. Now that kind of shit can happen over the phone. Don't we know anyone who could front as a buyer?"

"I don't know. And it would have to be a cash deal. But if I go into the bank and tell them a need a cashier's check for a good sum of money, and then the boat deal gets out, they'll know it's me."

"Stewart's got to know someone who could pull this together," said Sally.

"You're right. Let me call him."

So I did. He thought the plan was a good one, he loved the idea of what we were doing, but he didn't want us to get caught. I mean, it would just look really bad. Bad in a "these people have mental problems" way. So he got on the phone with Lyle Gugino, family friend, and get-it-done man, and within an hour a cashier's check was issued and being held at a New York City bank until further notice.

"So I guess all we have to do now is drive out and see this guy; make him an offer," I said.

"That's it. But we can't be us. God, maybe we should send someone else," said Sally. She was getting nervous and that was no good.

"No, way. We can't get anyone else involved in this. Look, we dress right, not too shabby, not too rich lady, and we get in Grant's truck and go down there.

And on the way, we'll come up with some bullshit story about why we want it."

"Okay. Tomorrow morning?"

"It'll be show time."

Arden and I spent the rest of the afternoon at the shop, playing with Jackson and listening to music. I told him I had some things to do the next morning, but that he should come back so he wouldn't be shut-up in the house, but apparently he'd made plans to help Stewart work on the boat. That was fine with me too; I just needed him out of the way. Before we left the shop I escaped to the office one more time to Google some things. I found what I needed as far as Arden and I were concerned, but it was a little more difficult for Sally. She and I might have to fly the coop for our treat.

When we got home that afternoon Stewart was out back firing up the grill so he could make us dinner, so Arden and I went to change into clothes that would allow us to eat more than we should. It had become a goal for Stewart to "fatten me up." And it was true that I'd lost a lot of weight after everything I'd been through, but having never been svelte in my entire life, I was kinda liking the thinner me. Stewart didn't mind it; he said he just missed my curves. But it was frustrating to all because none of my clothes fit. Shopper that I am, I couldn't bring myself to buy new clothes, always fearing that the weight would come back overnight. So even though I was somewhat svelte, or a reed, as Arden would say, I didn't dress the part.

I was a little fidgety during dinner, nervous about the next morning and wondering whether Sally and I could pull off this whole crazy idea. But it made me feel better to know that she was probably sitting around coming up with a great story to tell this old fisherman guy, because at the moment, all I could think about was the tasty filet mignon on my plate and the sun setting right before my eyes. It had been another good day.

The next morning I almost couldn't get out of bed. I think it was trepidation. I really wanted to do what I had planned, but I was getting nervous. I looked at my sleeping husband, thinking it would be nice to just lie next to him for another few minutes, and then I threw back the covers and dragged out of the bed. I knew that if I gave into the desire to snuggle with Stewart, I'd be in bed until noon, if not later. He had the effect of a blanket right out of the dryer, all warm and cozy. As I grabbed a pair of jeans from the closet, I glanced back over my shoulder one more time, but it wasn't going to do me any good to stand there and look at him, Sally was waiting. By the time I got out of the shower and got dressed Stewart was up and he and Arden were sitting in the kitchen having coffee. They were sharing sections of the paper like an old married couple.

"Hey cowgirl Viv, where are you off to today?" asked Arden.

"I'm sorry; didn't you get the press release? I'm not taking questions this morning," I said with a grin while pouring my coffee.

"I don't know which one of you is worse," said Stewart.

"Me," said Arden and I in unison.

"No, really, where are you going?"

"On an adventure with Sally."

"Well that means y'all could end up in Paris by this evening. But the cowboy boots don't work with that theory.'

"Then quit asking, because I'm not telling."

"Fine," said Arden with a touch of bitterness, which I knew was fake.

"Don't forget that Trosclair will be back this afternoon," said Stewart.

"I'll be back before then," I said, kissing both my boys on the forehead before I left. "Y'all have fun today."

I walked out to the driveway and got in my car, feeling a little better about the adventure. It was always fun to pull one over on Arden. He was usually the one to come up with this kind of shit. I put on some Violent Femmes and backed out of the driveway belting out *Prove My Love*. I made the left onto Lake Street and hauled ass to make the light at Lake and Sallier. Sally and Jack lived in 70605, and we made fun of them for it all the time. It didn't matter that she was only about five minutes from my house; it was a whole other world south of town.

The older houses were becoming few and far between as new subdivisions went up on any land available. I thought about that as I passed The Target. I was so glad we had it, but I wasn't pleased with the fact that a huge piece of land had to be cleared to build the shopping center it was a part of. I know, it sounds like a Joni Mitchell song, but it was true. And I guess The Target was nothing compared to the new casino. Talk about raping the land. But it does bring money into the economy, although sometimes I wonder just how much of that goes to the right place. It also brings in the Texans, but we won't go into that. I just tried to stay downtown as much as possible. Downtown I knew. I grew up riding my bike around the downtown area; going to the Civic Center and Sears, and sometimes Hardee's, when it was still Hardee's. But one of our favorite places was Maryanne's. And that made me think that Sally and I needed to be finished by lunch so we could indulge in one of their excellent burgers and some heavenly shoe-string onion rings. And that was the first thing I told her when she got in the car. She laughed, knowing how my mind wanders, but didn't ask what path I had taken to get there. We drove over to the marina to get Grant's truck; both of us a little nervous, and a little quiet, which was not normal. Of course Grant was out on a boat with a customer so I located the keys and we were off.

"Think we'll get away with it?" asked Sally. "If we do, it will be the best coup we have ever pulled off," I replied.

The Coup

The radio was on in the truck and Sally took it upon herself to find something to listen to. She ended up setting the dial on B103 so we could listen to the morning show that featured Justin and Amy. If anybody knew what anyone was saying about what was going on with Arden it would be those two. They are infamous at getting the word out.

"So, Amy, I guess you've heard about the pending trial for Arden Mercer?" Justin asked.

"Yes, Justin, and you know better than to ask me about things like that. I'm not supposed to cuss on the air. But I will say that I think it's all wrong. I went to high school with Arden, and I just don't think he's got it in him," said Amy.

"Listeners, tell us what you think. We'll start taking your calls right after these commercials," said Justin.

"Oh, that's just great," said Sally, "I can only imagine what people around here are gonna say."

"I don't think it will be bad, Sally. Arden has been too good to too many people in this town. And besides, most kids are in school, so there shouldn't be too many crank calls."

"Still, I don't think I can listen to it."

"Too bad, because we're gonna, at least for a few minutes."

And just like I thought, it wasn't bad. Of course there were a few people who thought he could have done it, but they also admitted that they didn't know him. I thought they should have kept their opinions to themselves, but what do I know. I just hoped that Arden and Stewart weren't listening to the radio. Like I said, it wasn't bad, but I didn't think that Arden needed to hear any of it. Then again, he always loves a good scandal, and that is what we had on our hands. A bona fide Lake Charles scandal. Not as bad as shooting someone in front of a bunch of witnesses, but way worse than recycling a Mardi Gras gown.

When Sally had heard enough she turned the dial and found the country station. We sat and listened to Toby Keith, *I Ain't as Good as I Once Was*. It made me feel better. I love Toby Keith, I just do. When the song was over we tried to figure out how we were going to play our roles. It wasn't easy. If we came across too knowledgeable, we'd blow it. But if we tried to be too hokey he'd know something was up when we offered to pay for a boat. It was gonna be tough.

I took as many back roads as possible, weaving through the industrial plant compounds until I thought I was in a good position to get on Highway 27. The truck would not arouse suspicion, but you could never be too careful. We followed Jack's directions until we were south of the Creole Nature Trail. From there it got a little tricky because we had to go slow to make sure we didn't miss our turn. Even though when we found it we still thought it was wrong. Nothing but dirt road as far as the eye could see. But we followed it; and followed it, and followed it. Just when we were thinking we *were* lost, we saw Mr. Trahan's shack on a small piece of land that jutted out into the water.

"This dude is living in his own private Idaho," I said. "On the ground like a wild potato and everything."

"No, shit. Don't go on the patio. It makes me wonder if anyone has been out here to barter with him yet."

"It could be good for us if we are the first. God, cross your fingers," I said, pulling the truck up in front of the shack, and throwing it into park. I pressed in the emergency brake; I had this unwarranted fear that the truck would sink, sitting on this soggy peninsula. We weren't even out of the truck when the old man approached us.

"What brings you ladies all the way out here?" he asked. He was older than dirt, and smelled like an igloo cooler full of crabs. His hands were gnarled and yellow, and he was bald as the day he was born. But his eyes were alert and very bright blue. I wasn't sure how much crap we could get past him.

"We heard you had a hide to sell," said Sally, taking the reigns.

"I got lots of hides. What kind are you interested in?"

"Alligator," I said.

"Well, well. Y'all must be looking to buy that killer alligator hide. Am I right?"

"Yes, sir. What are you asking for it?" I asked.

"More than anybody around here wants to pay," he said, sounding disgusted. "What y'all got? I only take cash."

"What we got," said Sally, "is a new boat waiting for you over at Sonnier's. Actually, it's not brand new, but it's a good boat. And it's all yours...if you can part with the hide."

"How'd y'all know about the boat?" he asked.

"It was in the paper," I explained. "The reporter who talked to you mentioned that you were selling the hide because you wanted a new boat. Is that right?"

"Well, yeah, but a little cash wouldn't hurt, either," he said with a sour pinch. This is when Sally and I exchanged a knowing glance. We figured even with the boat, he'd up the ante and we were prepared.

We'd brought one thousand dollars in cash, but we new after talking to this guy that he'd take half of that happily.

"How about $500 for all your trouble?" Sally asked. And you could see the wheels turning. But he knew he'd never get a better offer. He mulled over it for a minute, looking down at his feet and then up at the sky, like he was really pondering the deal, and then he said, "I guess that would be good. The $500 and the boat right?"

"Yes, sir. And Mr. Sonnier has the boat all ready for you, down at his marina." Sally went to the truck and came back with an envelope, which she gave to the man.

"Thank y'all kindly," he said. He slipped the envelope down inside his overalls, and added, "Let me go get that hide for y'all." Sally and I just smiled at each other, we'd done it. Now we just had to ask him nicely, without offending him, to not tell anyone who bought it, and we were prepared to give him the rest of the cash to make this happen.

"Here it is," he said with a proud smile. "Treated it myself, been doing it since I could reach the table. My own Daddy taught me. Might need to be thinned, 'pendin' on what you wanna do with it. Know a guy up near Natchitoches who does it, let me write down his number for ya." And he did.

"Thank you so much Mr. Trahan. You've been very helpful. But there is one more thing we'd like to ask of you. If any one should come around asking who you sold the hide to, could you just say you don't remember what we look like?"

"You ladies got a problem with the law?" he asked suspiciously. "I don't need the police out here. Sheriff's Department, whatever. I don't need any problems."

"No, sir, we just don't want anybody nosing around trying to get a look at it. You know how people can be," said Sally.

"Sure, sure, I understand. Don't usually like nobody down here at my house at all, but I had to make an exception, you know, with selling this hide."

"We'd really appreciate it," I said.

"Anybody asks, I didn't get no names and I don't remember no faces."

We shook hands with Mr. Trahan then and got in the truck to head home. Sally waited until we were at the end of the road, turning back onto 27 before she yelled, "WE DID IT!!!" And we had. Now we just had to keep it under wraps and get the hide to the right people in order to complete the mission. And we made it back to Lake Charles in time to get Maryanne's for lunch.

Sally called Jack and he met us at the house for lunch. We arrived laden with brown paper bags from Maryanne's and Stewart and Arden were grateful. We sat out back in the yard and ate until we couldn't move, Sally and Arden griping because they were gaining so much weight now that I could eat whatever I wanted. But I reminded them that that wouldn't last forever. We were all still sitting there, gluttonous, when we heard the gate to the back yard creak open. It was Jules Trosclair, and following him was a very stylish looking Asian guy and a beautiful dark-haired girl with fair skin and dark eyes.

"Hello, everyone," said Trosclair. "We rang the bell, but when no one answered I figured y'all were out back."

"Please, come and join us," I said, motioning to the empty chairs.

"Absolutely," said Jack, getting up from his chair, "I'm heading back to work." And he gave Sally a kiss and said his good-byes. Stewart brought over another chair and excused himself, too, taking the remnants of lunch with him.

"I'll be in the garage if anyone needs me." When they were settled, Trosclair introduced his assistants.

"This is Juan," he said, referring to the guy I thought was Asian. "And this is Gretchen." We all agreed it was nice to meet them, and I could see that Arden was particularly pleased to meet Gretchen. She was hot. Even I could see that. And even if you were a super model; this girl was going to make you feel inferior.

"So what's new?" asked Arden.

"Well, these guys are being stubborn. I found out this morning that they are not going to offer a plea. They want a trial."

"Well, that's good, because I wouldn't have taken a plea. I didn't push her. Hell, I'm the dumbass who tried to save her. What is wrong with them that can't they understand that?"

"They think it's all about money," said Juan. "My source said that they were going with a revenge motive because of the funneling that was going on."

"Your source?" I asked. It made me a little nervous that he might know someone who could find out about what Sally and I had done. There are some crazy people out there...I read Carl Hiaasen novels. Those kinds of people would threaten Mr. Trahan without thinking twice, and my bet would be that Mr. Trahan would sing like a bird.

"Oh, yes Ma'am. I discovered that if you go to law school in the state of Louisiana you almost certainly know someone who knows someone who works for someone. It isn't that hard to make connections. And I went to school with a guy who has a friend who works here in Lake Charles at the courthouse."

"And what about you?" I asked Gretchen, trying to change the subject.

"Well, I'm not a lawyer," she said. "I do investigative work. My job right now is to find the tourists from Arizona. It would be nice to know if they saw anything." I felt much better after hearing her answer because unless she had a serious dark side, I couldn't see her trying to shake down Mr. Trahan. She looked more like the kind of investigator who goes under cover to seduce white collar criminals.

"So there was another car in the lot," said Sally.

"I told y'all that. I just didn't remember anything about it," Arden reminded us.

"It's a lead that we are working on. If we can find these people, it could help. They may have seen something, or even heard Arden yelling. It could be the key to getting the charges dropped all together," said Trosclair.

"Then let's get working on it," I said. "We can start calling hotels from here, to see if they had any registered guests from Arizona."

"It's not that simple, Mrs. Wainwright. It might be better if we went there in person and explained the situation," said Juan.

"Look," said Sally, "you have your sources and we have ours. Let us make a few phone calls."

I laughed quietly at what Sally had said. We did have our connections, as we'd proved that very day. It felt strange sitting there with everyone like nothing was going on. Meanwhile, harboring this secret of great proportions. It was so much fun to have pulled it off that of course we wanted to let everyone in on it, but that just wasn't going to happen. We weren't sure at that point how Trosclair would have reacted, but we knew it wasn't something he would have recommended.

The Sad Cake

Sally and Gretchen headed inside to place some calls. I left Arden and Trosclair and Juan sitting out back discussing things the prosecution might ask. I should have stayed to listen, but I was getting tired. The day was beginning to take its toll. I went to find Stewart for a much needed hug, but when I got to the kitchen I heard a knock on the back door. I could see through the curtain that it was my neighbor Miss Shirley from Henry Street. Our backyards butted up together and over the last year or so Miss Shirley and I had become close. She had always been there with a kind word or some sweets; baking was her forte.

"Hey, darlin'," she said when I opened the door, "I brought you a Sad Cake. You remember my Grandbaby, Marasha, don't you?"

"Absolutely. I heard you made the cheerleading squad with my niece. Congratulations."

"Thank you, Miss Nevers."

"So what kind of cake is this, Miss Shirley?"

"It's a Sad Cake. I got the recipe from my *Ladies' Taste of Heaven Cookbook*, put out by the Ladies Auxiliary and Junior Daughters Court No. 141 of the Knights of Peter Claver. Thought y'all might like it. I know things haven't been all that bright over here lately. Mr. Arden still bunking with you?"

"Yes Ma'am. He really doesn't want to be at home alone right now, and I feel better having him here so I can keep a close eye on him, especially with his Mama gone."

"That's right; she's on that pilgrimage to Lourdes. Bless her heart, not being able to be here for that child."

"Well, we didn't really tell her everything that was going on, just that Marilyn had died."

"Nevers, you got to tell that woman the truth. She would be out of her mind if she knew what was happening here."

"That's why we haven't told her. And we still have a week or so until the trial; we're holding out for some good news. Hopefully we'll get some soon. We hired a good lawyer."

"Well, if you think you are doing the right thing, baby, I'm behind you. I got to run and bring this baby to cheerleading practice," she said, planting a big kiss on my cheek. "You tell your Mama I said hello. And that handsome Yankee husband of yours, tell him I'll make him a casserole this week, something special, just for him."

"He'll love that Miss Shirley. Thank you for the cake," I said, showing them out. I waved from the back door until they were almost to the sidewalk and then went to find my husband for that hug.

Stewart was in the garage working. It was his new thing; he'd discovered that he liked to build stuff. And he wasn't a master carpenter, but a couple of the pieces he'd finished were pretty nice. I came up behind him while he was sanding, and wrapped my arms around his waist. He was sweaty and smelled like wood, and stain, and outside and I loved it. I kissed him on the neck.

"What're you doing?" he asked.

"Nothing," I lied.

"Are you trying to start something, Nevers Clark?"

"Me? Never!" I exclaimed, while giving him my most earnest look, the one he found so appealing, the one he could never say no to. And that did it. He spun around fast and was kissing me before I could catch my breath. This was one of the reasons I married him. He was the absolute best kisser I'd ever come across. Stewart kissed with his whole body, he had to be pressed up against me; and his hands would hold my face gently, contradicting what the rest of him was doing. It always left me weak in the knees. Of course he could kiss me innocently on the cheek during the middle of the day and that would also leave me in the form of a big blob.

"Thank you," I said, when he finally released me. "I'll be going now."

"You little Manx. What are you up to? Coming in here and starting this?"

"Nothing, honestly. I was just feeling a little worn down, so I figured I'd come in and get kissed properly, by someone who knows how."

"Pretty girl, if you're tired you need to go and lie down. Don't wear yourself out. I mean it, you worry me."

"I'll lie down in a little while, but first I'm going to check in on Gretchen and Sally, see what they've found out. Oh, Miss Shirley dropped off a Sad Cake and she said she'll be making a casserole just for you this week. I think she's sweet on you."

"That's only because I fixed her fence," he said popping me on the bottom with a rolled up shop towel. "Now get out of here so I can finish what I'm doing." But I leaned in and gave him one more good kiss before I left.

I found Sally and Gretchen sitting at the computer desk. One look through the den assured me that Arden and the other two were still in the back yard. My house felt like a command post. It didn't bother me though, if it wasn't happening here it would be harder to be a part of, and I definitely wanted to know what was going on at all times. While I was standing there thinking Arden looked up, saw me, and flipped me the bird. I turned around and stuck my butt out at him. And when I turned to walk into the living room, I could see Arden and Trosclair and Juan all laughing.

"So where are we girls?" I asked when I came up on Sally and Gretchen.

"Well, Lily came through for us like I knew she would. We checked the little places first with no luck. And then I decided to call Lily and have her check at L'Auberge, and bingo, we got a family from Tucson, checked out the day of the mishap. Now all we have to do is make contact," said Sally.

"So let's call them up."

"Well, I was just explaining to Sally that might not be the best idea," said Gretchen. "It has been my experience that people are more apt to talk to you if you are standing in front of them. Plus you can get a better feel for what they're saying, you know whether it's the truth or not."

"Okay, so you go to Tucson and find these people?"

"Here's the problem with that...I am waiting for all the financials to come in and I have to interview the guy at the bank, the one y'all said was acting strangely. And I was thinking, it might be better if the two of you talked to this family, you know on a personal level. Lots of people in a case like this don't want to come forward or get involved. It may take some persuasion on the part of the asker."

"I don't know if Nevers is up for that kind of traveling," said Sally.

"What about you? Who would take care of Jackson? And what would we tell people? We certainly don't want everyone to know what we are doing," I said.

"Here's my idea," said Gretchen. "Everyone knows your health has been an issue, right Nevers? If anyone should ask, we'll tell them that you were feeling run down, so Stewart sent you off to a spa in Tucson for a couple of days. They have this place, The Canyon Ranch; we could say you went there. And if we say it was Stewart's idea and Arden approved I don't think anyone would argue."

"It sounds good, and it would feel good to get these people to talk to us. Sally, do you think you could get away?"

"Yeah, Jack will make it happen. He'd want me to go. And I can line up Miss Shirley and your Mama as back-up."

"So I guess we're going to Tucson," I said.

"Yep, we're headed for the desert."

The only problem I had, after looking at a map of Tucson was where we were supposed to stay. The Spa was way out in bum-fuck-Egypt, as we used to say in high school about people who lived in Moss Bluff. Sally and I thought it best if we stayed in the city, and I remembered a place mentioned in *Vanity Fair*; The Arizona Inn. It was right by UMC hospital and the University of Arizona campus, and it sounded perfect. Built in the thirties, it was quaint and private, and as Arden would say, Rich Lady. He was probably going to be jealous. I left Sally and Gretchen to make the reservations and went to make a pot of coffee, shamed that I hadn't thought of it before for our guests. I hollered at Stewart to meet us out back and I carried a tray with the coffee and the Sad Cake across the manicured lawn.

I could tell that Stewart was a little worried about my making the trip, but he knew that Sally wouldn't let me over do it. And Trosclair looked concerned, but for different reasons, I'm sure. Arden was jealous of the whole Arizona Inn thing, but I promised him a trip when all of this was over. Juan had a friend who practiced law in Tucson and offered to make a call in case we needed any legal aid. Sally and Gretchen came out to meet us, informing the crew assembled that we were to leave the next morning. And then we all had some Sad Cake, which was surprisingly cheerful.

Maybe it was the fact that we felt like we were making head-way. If these people actually saw or heard something useful, we could create some reasonable doubt or maybe even get the charges dropped all together. It might have been wishful thinking, but as Molly Ringwald said in *Sixteen Candles*, when you've got nothing, you've got nothing to lose, right? Even though that was kind of harsh. We might not have much, but neither did the prosecution. Sure, Marilyn was moving money around, but that alone didn't mean that Arden killed her. And that was really all they had. They could say the marks on her arm were from a struggle, but Arden had already admitted to the fact that he was trying to pull her to safety. It wasn't even he-said-she-said, because Marilyn wasn't here to say anything.

As the Sad Cake worked its magic, the afternoon found us, this peculiar mix of people, actually relaxing and having as good a time as could be had under the circumstances.

The Detective

I still could not get over what I had done. If anything got out about Eva and me, it would be the end of the road as far as my career is concerned. This was the thought running through my mind while I sat at my desk and wondered what to do next. I had tried calling Eva, but either she wasn't home, or she didn't want to talk to me. It wasn't that I didn't want what happened to happen, because I did. I just wish I would have had the brains to wait until all this Arden Mercer crap was over.

The problem with the case is that it should have never started. I've had front row seats from the very beginning and the plot still doesn't make any sense to me. They keep saying that Arden murdered his wife because he found out she was stealing from him, but I just don't buy it.

From what I can tell Arden Mercer is a smart guy, no matter what Marilyn had put him through, he still wouldn't have done it this way. He hit me as more of a public humiliation kind of guy, you know, the kind that would drag her name through the mud and ruin her socially. But my opinion apparently doesn't matter. The Sheriff won't listen to any argument that goes against his theory. I kept wondering, if Cameron Parish had kept this case would it be proceeding like this? And the answer I kept coming up with was, no way. It is my theory that if Cameron Parish had held their ground, this would be over. They would have written it off as an accident. And not because they are incompetent, but because it had to be true. They should have stood their ground.

The more time I spent working on this case, the more intrigued I became as to why we were going forward with it. So I decided to start doing some side-line investigating. But first I had to talk to Eva.

Since I had tried her house and the flower shop where she worked and hadn't had any luck, I decided to go straight to the source; RPM's. I knew that Nevers Wainwright's music store was a hang-out, and I thought maybe Eva was hanging there. And I could go under the guise of investigating. It was true that I hadn't yet talked to Kiki or Wes, and they know Arden. And if Eva happened to be there, so much the better. It was still early, though, so I thought it would be a good time to start my side-line investigating. The first thing I did was to Google the Sheriff. I typed in 'Francis Arceneaux', and to my surprise I got a couple of hits; most of it pertained to his career in the Sheriff's Department, but there were a couple of entries from an alumni website that touted his high school football skills.

But his glory days didn't last long. An injury his senior year smashed any hopes of playing for LSU, which was his dream. Being a guy, I know what kind of effect that can have on your life. I thought it was smart not to ask the Sheriff about it, but to question other people who knew him at the time. I started with a phone call to Ronny Johnson, a retired state trooper who had known Sheriff Arceneaux all his life.

"Boy, do I remember that night," said Mr. Johnson.

"What exactly happened?"

"Arceneaux was preoccupied. Never did know how to separate himself from what was going on and just play. Got tackled by this big ol' kid from Jennings, and when they fell the kid landed on Frank's knee the wrong way. It was ugly, I'll tell you that. But now I got a question for you. Why all the interest in your boss's old glory days?"

"We're thinking about throwing a little party for him," I lied, "you know, celebrating his 16th anniversary with the department. I thought it might be cool to do a little 'This Is Your Life' thing." I was glad I still had the Google page in front of me; otherwise I'd have never known how long the Sheriff had been with the department.

"Well, I wouldn't go dragging up this football bullshit. He never really got over it. You know what I mean?"

I knew what Mr. Johnson meant. He meant, if you ever want to piss off your boss, start talking about the game against Jennings that ended his football career. My question was: why was the Sheriff preoccupied? What in the world could have made someone so intent on playing the game lose his concentration? Here was the mystery. I didn't know if I was capable of finding the answer without pissing him off, but I was sure going to try. I left the office about ten, letting them know I was going to conduct some interviews. What I didn't tell them was that I was going to find out if my job was at stake. Yeah, I was going to question people, but it didn't have anything to do with Arden Mercer.

When I pulled up in front of RPM's I could tell there were people inside, I just couldn't tell who it was. Since Pujo Street was one way, I parked on the north side of the street so I wouldn't be right in front of the door. I was nervous, and I hated it. I needed to find Eva to make sure things had not been broadcast, but at the same time I wanted to know if she thought what had happened was a mistake. And if she did, well, it was gonna hurt. I don't think anyone heard me coming into the store. Kiki was behind the counter sorting some papers and singing *Son of a Preacher Man* at the top of her lungs, and she was rocking it with a beautifully strong gospel choir voice.

"Hey good-looking," she sang, changing her tune. "Whatcha got cooking?"

"Hey, yourself. It's Kiki, right?" I said this even though I remembered. I wanted her to think she'd made an impression the first time. "I wanted to talk to you and Wes, that's his name, right, the guy who works here? Well, I wanted to ask y'all a few questions about Mr. Mercer."

"Well, if it isn't Mr. Headboard," said a tall, lanky guy coming from a back room. This had to be Wes. Tight skinny jeans and an old Social Distortion t-shirt (the real deal, not the kind you can buy at Hot Topic) made up his outfit, accented with a pair of Chuck Taylor's that had seen better days.

"I'm sorry, what was that about a headboard?" And the minute I said it I remembered. We'd laughed when it happened, but it wasn't all that funny to me now. These people knew. Immediately I felt bad for Eva.

"Look, super cop, I know y'all were drunk, but come on."

"Well, my question as to whether or not anyone found out about us has been answered. Is Eva here?"

"Why should we tell you, Sucka?" asked Wes in a smart-ass hip-hop way.

"Back down, child," said Kiki, "let me handle this. Just what is it you want with our girl? She didn't do anything wrong. Unless getting drunk and sleeping with a cop is a crime. But last I heard, it wasn't. Have things changed?"

"I'm the only one who can get in trouble for that. I just want to talk to her. "

"Oh, my God! Look Kiki, he's hot for Eva!" said Wes, pointing at me like I was on fire.

"Yeah, I see it. But is it for real?"

"If you must know, it's real. But I wouldn't call it 'the hots'. And I don't know why I'm telling y'all this anyway. This is crazy."

"Not really. Shit like this happens all the time in here. See me and Kiki are all about keeping it real."

"And the stuff you say in here doesn't go past those front doors," said Kiki.

"Yeah, we're like Vegas," agreed Wes. "Only, it's a lot cleaner here."

"Y'all leave him alone," said another voice, one that I recognized, from the back of the store. "Hey, Detective. What are you doing here?"

"Eva. I just wanted to talk to you. I wasn't able to reach you at home, so I thought I'd try here. I hope I'm not causing too much trouble." I felt like such a dumb ass, explaining my presence. I wondered where the no-nonsense cop had gone. But to be honest, he checked out the minute Eva smiled at him across the bar. This girl was the real thing.

"Come back to the office for a minute. We can talk in peace back here." I followed her to the back of the store and into a little room cluttered with paperwork and shipping invoices. She closed the door and asked me to have a seat.

"I'm really sorry, Eva."

"Sorry for what?"

"For the way things went. It's not my style to take a drunk girl home and, well…"

"And well, what? You didn't take advantage of me if that's what you think. I'm a big girl, Ezra. I knew what I was doing."

"I didn't mean for it to come out that way. Look, I'm here because I like you Eva, I really do. But it couldn't have come at a worse time for me. If anybody from work were to find out what happened, I could lose my job."

"Look, my friends know, but they're not going to say anything. They'll look out for me, because we really don't need any more of a scandal than what we're dealing with now."

"That's good to know. But there's something else. I want you to know that when this case is closed I want to see you again. The right way. I want us to go out to dinner, and see movies. You know? Regular dating stuff."

"Well, it doesn't sound like as much fun as the other night, but we can give it a shot," she said with a grin. And I was smitten.

I left RPM's feeling the best I've felt since this Arden Mercer thing started. If nothing leaked out, I was in the clear until this mess was over. But until then I decided to get the ball rolling on my own. My first stop was Lake Charles Boston High School, Sheriff Arceneaux's Alma Mater. Surely they'd have some old yearbooks lying around there. And if I was lucky, I just might find some more people I could talk to. I wasn't sure why I felt the way I did about my boss. But his insistence bothered me. Call it Detectives' Intuition; it just felt like something was up.

Go West, Young Ladies

I hated flying out of Lake Charles. Continental was the only option, and I was not a big fan of Continental. But with the short notice on this trip, it really was better than driving to Houston. And once we got to Intercontinental, we'd be switching to American anyway. Sally and I had packed as light as we could. Jeans, comfy shoes, sweaters. We really weren't sure what the weather would be like and everyone I'd spoken to reminded me that the desert nights and mornings were cool, and layers were the best way to go. After an uneventful flight, we landed in Tucson.

We rented a car, a sassy new convertible Mustang, got directions from the Hertz guy, and headed out. It was a good thing we had a city map, though, because once out of the airport we got a little turned around. We ended up on Palo Verde, which turned into Alvernon, which went up to Speedway, which then took us to Campbell, which is where we needed to be. We probably saw more of the city than necessary, but it was fun. I was amazed at how pretty the city is. Having lived in Vegas, I knew how dirty the desert could be, but Tucson was different. It is very well maintained with beautiful landscaping on all the major roadways, and the surrounding mountains are gorgeous.

Sally was impressed, also. I could tell. Tucson reminded us a little of Baton Rouge, and so we dubbed it The Baton Rouge of the West. It was a big college town with lots of money, but it also had a side less fortunate. Tucson is a huge immigrant town, and this was evident everywhere you looked. We got to the Arizona Inn without too much trouble, and went inside to check in. We were impressed with the accommodations; the guest suite we'd reserved was beautiful, as were the grounds.

And the minute we got to the front desk we had info regarding our quest. It seems Juan's friend had found the family we were looking for. We called him immediately.

"It might be a little more difficult than we thought," said Miguel Xavier Lopez, Esquire. "The guy is active duty military, stationed at Davis Monthan Air Force Base here in town. Now, I can get us on base, my Dad is retired military and I have an ID, but it is going to be up to you two to get him to talk to us." I was a little frightened by the whole military aspect of it. I mean, being from Lake Charles, we had contact with the military, but those were Army guys who came to town to drink and have fun. This guy was a Tech Sergeant in the United States Air Force.

"What kind of job does he do?" I asked, hoping he wasn't some Special Operations kind of guy.

"He's a Black Hawk mechanic. From what I could find out, he's pretty down to earth, but he hasn't mentioned anything to his friends or co-workers about witnessing an alligator mauling while in Louisiana."

"Great, that means he doesn't want to be involved in any of this," said Sally. It was the same thing I had been thinking.

"Well, it's still worth a shot," I said. "We didn't come here for nothing. I'll make the call this evening and see if he'll talk to us."

We had some time on our hands so after we showered and changed we asked Marisela, the beautiful Hispanic girl with gorgeous green eyes who worked at the front desk, where we should eat. She suggested Casa Sanchez on 22nd Street; she said they had the best chimichanga in town. We found it easily. One good thing about Tucson, it is pretty much a square grid city. And we found that Marisela did not lie. We had, quite possibly, the best chicken chimichanga in the world. We sat there, stuffed, still eating chips with homemade salsa, discussing the best way to find out what this Tech Sergeant knew.

"I think that I should just be as honest as possible. I mean Arden is our best friend, our brother, surely this guy can understand that. He's military; they are all about standing by each other. He's just got to understand how important this is."

"He may understand, Nevers, but that doesn't mean he'll talk about it. I mean maybe they didn't see anything at all, and that's why he never came forward. This is a crap-shoot, at best. I know we have to ask, that's what we came here to do, but I don't want you getting your hopes up. This could be a dead end."

That night, when I made the call, I was scared to death. Talking to this guy, this Sgt. Michael Edwards was so important to me, and I was frustrated and crying. I explained that Arden was my best friend, that we'd grown up together, and that what had happened was a tragedy, but that we knew Arden didn't have anything to do with it, and that we were scared because the Sheriff's Department was pushing so hard to get it to trial.

And here's the thing…when I mentioned the trial, he got confused, said he hadn't heard anything about that. Maybe the guy felt sorry for me, maybe he could hear the desperation in my voice. I don't know what it was, but he agreed to see us. I explained our situation with Miguel and Sgt. Edwards was okay with him being there, so it was settled. Tomorrow, one o'clock, the food court at the Base Exchange. After a restless night, Sally and I ordered breakfast in.

We felt kind of bad about not getting out and seeing more of the city while we had time, but we were too nervous. We took our time getting ready that morning, the only interruption a phone call from Eva. We put her on speaker phone.

"What're y'all doing?" she asked, with child-like curiosity, which could only mean that something was up.

"Eating breakfast and watching *Amelie* on the IFC. You know Nevers. I think she's in love with that Audrey girl," said Sally.

"Shut-up," I said.

"What's up at home? How's Jackson?" asked Sally.

"Everything is good. Jackson hung out with us at the shop for a while yesterday, Jack had to go meet with a client, but that's not why I'm calling. Listen, Ezra thinks he has a line on the Sheriff," said Eva.

"What are you talking about?" I asked.

"Well, you know he can't come out and say it, but I think even Ezra thinks that the charges are full of shit. So he figures the Sheriff has a bone to pick, so he started to do a little digging. Did you know that Sheriff Arceneaux dated Miss Lorelei in high school?"

"Excuse me?" said Sally, she was eating a croissant and almost choked.

"Are you serious? Does Arden know this?" I asked.

"Not that I know of. Ezra is just kind of playing around with theories at this point. He only told me because...well, he needed a sounding board, and he knew he couldn't go to anyone in the department."

"It kind of sounds like that six degrees of separation thing; you know the Kevin Bacon thing. But even if he dated her, what does that prove?" asked Sally.

"He doesn't really even know, at this point. I just thought I'd let y'all know what was going on. Oh, and I have some other news, so let me tell you and then you can proceed to laugh and then I'll let you go…Someone bought that alligator hide. Can you believe that? And the old guy who had it won't say who it was." Sally and I just looked at each other and smiled. That little bit of information, for some strange reason, put us in a better mood. The way I figured it, if we could pull that off, we could do almost anything.

By the time Miguel came to get us, we were more than ready to go. There was some good gris-gris in the air and we could feel it. I was still a little confused by the information about the Sheriff, but that would have to wait until later to be processed. We loaded into Miguel's mini Hummer, which was pretentious and embarrassing; I really didn't want to be seen in it, but he had the vehicle pass to get on base. Taking Speedway down to Craycroft, we got to see a little more of the city. The University was west of us, however, so we didn't see that.

The stop light outside of the gate looked like any other in town, except for the fact that in the cars next to you there were people in uniform, and when you crossed Golf Links, it was a whole different world. Miguel used the right lane and pulled into the Visitors Center so we could get passes. He handed his ID and our drivers licenses to the Airman behind the counter. The guy asked where we were going. Miguel told him, "The BX." And after getting Miguel's phone number the Airman pushed all our stuff back, including two white slips of paper which resembled hall passes. This was a whole new thing for us. It was kind of an exclusive thing, very rich lady.

The only thing we could liken it to was signing someone in at the Racquet Club. And even then, they didn't get a pass.

We drove up the road to the BX, the Base Exchange, run by Aafes, (Army and Air Force Exchange Services). The Navy has the NEX, the Navy Exchange; and the Marines have the MCX, the Marine Corps Exchange. I'm not sure why the Army and the Air Force are lumped together, but on an Army Post it's called the PX. There's really no difference, but Miguel said that you should always call it by the proper exchange name. It was crowded, and there were lots of older people there. Miguel explained that Davis Monthan was a big "snowbird base", a warm place in the winter for retirees to flock to. "They come in their RV's in the winter and stay until it starts to get really hot. Then I guess they go somewhere like Montana. Who knows." When we got out of the car, Sally and I were mesmerized by the amount of cute boys in uniform; they were everywhere. We must have looked like outsiders, however, because when we walked into the food court Sgt. Edwards noticed us immediately. Maybe it was the whole southern-women-accompanied-by-the-local-Hispanic-attorney thing, but he knew who we were. He came over and introduced himself, and then led us to an out of the way table by the front windows. The lunch crowd was thinning out, and it was pretty quiet in our corner.

"Let me first say that I didn't know anything about charges being brought," he explained, "otherwise we would have come forward."

"Sgt. Edwards, may I record this conversation? If we get what we need, it *could* mean that charges *could* get dropped and you'd never have to testify," said Miguel.

"Yeah, I want to clear this up. I feel bad because we left, but you have to understand. We, my wife and I, were there with our four-year-old son. We were just walking around, having a good time; my son had been chasing rabbits, when we came around a bend that allowed us to see back to where we had been. Up until that point we didn't even know that anyone else was there. We never heard another voice until we heard the scream," he said.

"Marilyn's scream," said Sally.

"No, it was the guy, your friend Arden. I don't think the girl made any noise. It happened really fast. We saw them standing there, and then it looked like she bent down, and then after a while it looked like he reached down to help her up, and then he screamed. When we saw the water churning and splashing, we ran. We knew exactly what it meant; the water churning like it was. I know it was wrong, but the only thing we could think about was our son's safety. We did call 911, though. It wasn't possible for us to just leave that poor guy out there alone. Then we went back to the hotel and we left, as scheduled, the next day."

"Wow," I said. It sounded stupid, but it was the only thing that came out of my mouth. We'd only heard the story from Arden, and he was so emotionally attached, it was hard to visualize. Hearing Sgt. Edwards tell it, it took on the quality of a movie scene. It was infinitely more shocking.

I tried, once again, to imagine what Arden had gone through that day. There was the wonderful feeling that morning that things were starting to go well, then the shock of the attack. And I know it haunted him, but there was that one moment he spoke about when everything seemed clear to him. Being raised the same; I know that Arden felt guilt for what happened. How could anyone stand there and watch that happen and not feel guilt. But I also knew that the more we learned about Marilyn, the more her personality was revealed, the less guilt there was to go around.

The Military Tourist

Man, I felt so bad for these women. Fighting the system is never fun. I was glad I had something to tell them, but I didn't really know if it would help. I'd seen people get screwed before. When we, my wife and I, saw what happened that day, we were wishing we were someplace else. Now I'm kind of glad we were there. One thing I got from those women is that they care about their friend, and I admire anyone who will fight for what they believe in. And they believe in their friend. But the whole situation was still strange. I'm a city boy, myself.

I was raised in Houston. And I mean *in the city* as my parents never ventured farther than that. That separated me from what they, Nevers and Sally, knew of nature. That was part of the reason I joined the military. To see something other than the city. But I should have done better research. Almost all Air Force bases are located in cities; there is nothing remote about them. I guess if I wanted to play in the woods I should have gone Army or Marines. But my chances of getting shot at were lower in the Air Force and I had a wife and a baby on the way when I joined, so there you go.

Our trip home had been a really good one. We'd spent some time in Houston with my parents, going to museums and restaurants. My Mother took Halley, my wife, out shopping. My Dad and I took my son to the driving range with us. That was as close to nature as it got with my Dad. We decided after a couple of days to drive over to Westlake, Louisiana to visit Halley's Grandparents, and they suggested we take our son, Sam, out to the Creole Nature Trail.

"It's beautiful out there," her Grandfather told us. Of course they warned us of the alligators and such. But no one, and I mean no one, had ever heard of anyone ever being attacked. And Halley's Grandparents were right, it is beautiful out there, certainly like nothing else I had ever seen. Halley hadn't been there since she was a kid, so we were really enjoying ourselves. Sam loved seeing the alligator crossing signs, and the bridges we had to cross. The sky was endless where it touched the water. I understood immediately why people would choose to live their lives there; it had that much of an effect on me.

When we arrived we didn't see any other cars in the lot, but Halley said they may have parked on other turn-offs and walked over. We got out the bug repellant and slathered it on every exposed part of our bodies, knowing that the mosquitoes could eat you alive. Halley got the camera out and I grabbed an insulated bag that had water and snacks for Sam. After double checking that shoes were tied, and the car was locked we headed towards the start of the trail. It was still early enough to not be too hot, but the humidity was high. Of course that was normal, just not to us. After being in the dry heat of Tucson for awhile, the humidity will throw you off, make it hard to catch your breath. But we were keeping it slow for Sam anyway. He is a naturally curious four-year-old.

Like I said before, we didn't know if anyone else was there. So it surprised us when we made the turn that I told Nevers and Sally about, and there were their friends. What was surprising is that it is naturally quiet out there, so all we'd been hearing was the wind and the birds. Occasionally you'll hear a boat, but even those aren't loud. So not having heard two adults, who were not that far behind us, threw me off a little. Maybe that is part of the reason I stopped to watch them. That and the fact that they were standing so close to the water.

We'd been told by everyone we talked to not to do that. Apparently, even though alligators look cumbersome, they are quick. I think back on it now and wonder if I heard the low rumbling, the water vibrations, or if it was just in my head. Surely the sound couldn't have traveled that far.

The whole scene has stayed with me. It was like a car crash and I couldn't look away. And I will always feel guilt for not sticking around and helping the guy, but we were scared for our son. And at that point I didn't know anything about Arden Mercer which meant that my son came first. When we realized what was happening I swung my son up on my hip and we stared running. When we got to the car, scared and out of breath, we called 911. I felt like it was all I could do. We left because we knew if we stayed that we'd be there all day. The cops would want information and I wasn't about to have my son standing on the side of the road all day while my wife and I were interrogated.

Like I said, I put my family first. At least that's the way I justify it. But really, once that woman went in the water there wasn't anything I could do. And I seriously doubted the alligator would go after the guy. That was my reasoning. We were leaving the next day anyway, so we packed up and headed back to Houston late that afternoon. When my son did ask about what happened, we told him that people had been playing in the water and we didn't want to be there if they stirred up the alligators. He said, "Yeah, that would be scary." He thought the whole thing was an adventure. We let him believe that.

I'm still not sure how the people in Lake Charles found us, but Halley reminds me all the time about small towns. She grew up in Dequincy, Louisiana, and she would know. And I wasn't sure what to expect when I met Nevers and Sally, but I think they were good people. You could tell they had money, but they weren't flashy. Like they didn't want to be better than anyone else, and I liked that. I don't know much about fashion either, but I do know that Nevers had a shirt on that came from Target. I know because my wife has the same shirt. That made them real to me. That and their devotion to their friend. When Nevers said that it sounded like a scene from a movie I agreed with her, it had felt that way for us too.

I know that it made them feel better, hearing what I had to say. You could see them relax a little, Sally even asked to see a picture of my son and she and Nevers oooh'ed and ahhh'd over him. It was like they finally let out a big breath that they'd been holding for too long. They even mentioned going to look at Coach bags inside the store. I felt better too. If what I knew helped them, then I wasn't too late. And I would have come forward if I'd known anything about the charges, and they knew that now. So I left them to go look at purses, thinking that Louisiana girls were some of the best girls around. That's why I married one.

Arden

It is really boring in Lake Charles when Nevers and Sally are gone. Not to say that Stewart and I weren't having a good time. We were. But even Stewart understands that sometimes things are way more funny when Nevers and Sally are laughing. I've been in and out of meetings with Trosclair and his posse (as Stewart calls them) for the last two days, and I know that I need to concentrate, but *really*. The sensationalism has died down and this case has just become boring. Maybe it's because I know I didn't push Marilyn to her death. And honestly, the money was nothing. Sure, it was a big hit, but there is still money around that she never even knew about.

I decided that I needed to take stock of things, to see how I really felt about what had happened, and there was only one place to do that. And I hadn't been there in what felt like months, when in reality it has only been days. So I got into Nevers' Mini Cooper, turned down the Franz Ferdinand blaring from her speakers, and drove over to my house. I don't know what I was expecting to find, other than a full mailbox and maybe a UPS notice or two. My cars were covered in pollen, naturally. I hadn't expected any less. But sometimes it's nice to think that there could be a car wash fairy, who buffs and waxes while you are away. Like Nevers dreams of Immaculate Waxing, where you wake up and your bikini line is DONE. But there had been none of that. Which was depressing. I love my house, and I still considered it *my* house; to be frank, Marilyn just wasn't here all that much, she never left her mark so to speak.

All Marilyn wanted to do was get out of Lake Charles; there was no planting of the roots for her. From the very beginning, that was her plan. She would have stayed in

LA the first time we went if it wasn't for me. And I am always loving a glamorous lifestyle, but not twenty-four-seven. While Marilyn and I were married, I got sick of fancy hotel rooms, and dragging around to parties. It is a very pretentious world, and you don't see that side of it on television. I was just so taken with Marilyn at that point that I went along. And now it is so easy to throw those feelings away, and that's a little frightening. But she really brought it on herself, what with her lies and deceit. There were now things that I didn't know about her that I wasn't really sure I wanted to know.

Like the whole issue of her parents. What is that about? She could have told me she grew up in foster homes; it might have gotten her a little respect. You know, that she came from that environment and made her way to the top. Now it was just another big fat lie to deal with. And I guess I'll never know what the money bit was about. She'd made a small fortune when she sold her screenplay, I couldn't imagine what she needed more money for. And I was sick of thinking about it. I walked under the carport and used my key to open the back door. It wasn't as sticky as usual because there hadn't been too much rain, but once I got inside things did smell a little musty.

It was like walking onto the set of a movie. The big round ashtray that Nevers loves was still in the middle of the table, and our coffee cups from that wretched morning were in the sink. I really expected to see at least one roach, but there were none. Maybe they didn't want to be here either. I crossed into the living room, and there was still a pile of CD's on the floor from the night before Marilyn's demise. I had stayed up late listening to music after Marilyn went to bed. I loved doing that. Nevers and I used to do that; drink too much and get hooked on one song. Nevers would usually dance around for a while, but eventually we'd end up lying around on the floor, or the couch, and the next morning, we'd be in the same place.

But that last night with Marilyn had been different. "I'm not listening to this shit anymore," she'd said, stomping off to bed. And I let her go. I really wasn't in the mood for her crap. That is why I was a little surprised the next morning when she was so gung-ho about getting out and doing something. I was glad, but hesitant. I'd seen that side of Marilyn before, but not very often. It usually only came out when she wanted something which was confusing. I couldn't figure out what she had to gain by going to the Creole Nature Trail. And then it hit me. What if her plan all along was to do to me what actually befell her?

All of the sudden the room felt like it was spinning. It couldn't possibly be true, but it was something to think about. I gathered my senses and walked back to the bedroom where the few things she had were kept in a big, red Rubbermaid storage tote. I yanked that thing from the closet and started dragging out all its contents. I found the original copy of her screenplay, a bunch of receipts from her last trip to Neiman's in Houston, and a small, black leather journal. She'd been keeping notes on meetings with the studio people and script changes, which was normal. But towards the back she was outlining what looked to me like another screenplay. And the plot was all too familiar.

I carefully replaced everything I'd drug out and put the box back in the closet. I didn't want anyone to know what I'd found, you know that whole saying about action and reaction. I wasn't sure what the reaction would be so I decided to keep the journal under wraps until Nevers and Sally got back. They'd know what to do with it. I didn't bother to go through the rest of the house; Marilyn's presence had been contained in that box. When all of this was over and I couldn't be accused of destroying evidence, I'd get rid of the box, and have my cleaning lady Carmelita give the house a good sanitizing.

Too Much Information

I felt kind of bad for not staying in Tucson longer, but Sally and I both felt we should really get home with the information we had. So after meeting with Sgt. Edwards we went back to the room and called the airline to change our tickets.

"We'll be sleeping in our own beds tonight," said Sally. "But we'll have to drive home from Houston. We arrive too late to get a connection."

"That's okay. Let's get our shit together and get out of here."

And by 1:30 am central time, we were pulling into the driveway at my house. Stewart and Arden were both on the porch, sitting in the rocking chairs waiting for our arrival. The light wasn't on, but you could see the tip of Arden's cigarette glowing from the car. Stewart came over to help with my bag, and Arden went to the driver's window to talk to Sally. I could tell they were planning something, I just didn't know what. I leaned in and kissed Sally goodnight and she headed home.

"What's with the James Bond aura?" I asked Arden when we were alone. Stewart had headed to bed, which really meant he was lying in there watching *Sex and the City* reruns.

"I found something at the house, in Marilyn's things," he said, playing it cool. We were sitting at the kitchen table, and I got up to grab a can of Coke from the icebox, knowing it wouldn't keep me up in my exhausted state.

"What kind of something?"

"Well, I won't go into too many details tonight; we have a brunch meeting scheduled for tomorrow. But

I will say that I no longer feel any guilt for anything that happened."

"You've been exonerated? I don't understand. We got what we needed in Tucson. What could you have possibly found at your house that would clear you?" It was late, and I was sleepy and getting confused.

"It doesn't clear me as far as the cops go, but I no longer have a guilty conscience. Look, I'll explain tomorrow. You go on to bed."

And with that he got up, kissed my forehead and headed for the guest room. Everyone slept late the next day. And as usual, I was the first one up at my house. I had just started the coffee pot when I heard a faint knock on the back door. It was Jules Trosclair. I had no idea what he was doing on my back porch this early, and then I remembered it wasn't early. Arden had said something about him coming over so it wasn't an altogether unexpected visit. I opened the door and greeted him as gracefully as possible considering I had dog breath.

"Nevers, I am so sorry to be here this early. I know you and Mrs. LaFleur only returned late last night, but have news that can't wait." A normal person would've sounded flustered, but not Jules.

"It's not early, Mr. Trosclair."

"Jules, please."

"Okay, Jules," I said with a smile. He was revved up about something, and I figured I should placate him. "But really, it's not early. We just got in late. I'm confused, though. Arden wanted us, me and Sally and Stewart, to be available at eleven this morning but he didn't say anything about you being here."

"Well, I guess I wasn't invited, but this news couldn't wait. We finally got the bank guy, what's his name? Crap, I can't remember. Pardon my French."

"Elliot. And you'll hear much worse from my mouth so don't sweat it. I guess I should go get those guys up." And just as I said it, Stewart came wandering into the kitchen in his underwear. He looked at Trosclair, said, "Oops" and walked back out. Since I was in my nightgown with just a t-shirt thrown over it, I excused myself as well. "Please help yourself to coffee. We'll be with you shortly."

I went to get Arden up first and discovered him gone. I was a little worried so I called him only to find out that he'd been up since dawn and was now sitting in the drive-thru at Nelson's donuts. I told him Trosclair was here so he better get plenty. By the time I washed my hair and brushed my teeth and went back to the kitchen the coffee pot was almost empty and Stewart and Jules were deep into conversation. From what I could gather, Jules knew the best fishing spots on any water in south Louisiana, and Stewart was looking forward to tagging along the next time Jules went out.

"When this show closes, we'll plan a weekend trip. We can cover a lot of ground in a weekend," said Jules.

"It sounds like heaven, Jules. I'm looking forward to it. But I'm also looking forward to closing the book on this Arden thing. The stress is taking a toll on my wife," said Stewart like I wasn't standing there. So I whacked him on the back of the head. "Well, it is. What am I supposed to do? Lie?"

"No, but you shouldn't talk about me like I'm not in the room."

"Sorry," he said a little sheepishly.

"It's okay. Look, Arden is on his way back from Nelson's, and Sally should be here any minute. Let's move this party to the dining room."

I made another pot of coffee and we headed into the dining room. Trosclair, pardon me, Jules pulled out a big file and laid it out on the table. We were ready and waiting for Sally and Arden to show up. Sally came in first, Jackson on her hip. We all fawned over the baby until Arden sashayed in about ten minutes later, then Sally and I went to put up the port-a-crib and got Jackson settled. We made small talk for a while, everyone much more enjoying the donuts and coffee than the task at hand.

"Arden, you go first," said Sally. "I want to know what you found at the house."

"What is she talking about?" asked Trosclair.

"Well, I went home yesterday to check on things. You know, I got the mail and I had every intention of cleaning up a little, but as I was standing there thinking things through, the strangest thought came to me. What if Marilyn had dragged me down to Cameron to kill me? What if it was her intention all along?

I mean, she'd never mentioned going there before, and the night before she was her regular self, bitching about the music I was listening to, and then stomping off to bed in her mules. How did it come to pass that she was in such a good mood the next morning?"

"Arden do you really think that she wanted to kill you?" asked Stewart.

"Well, I wasn't sure until I found this," he said pulling out a black leather-bound journal. "It looks like an outline, maybe for a new screenplay, but I don't think that's what it is. I think it is a plan, written in the form of an outline, to throw off anybody who might read it."

"May I?" asked Trosclair, reaching for the journal. He was tentative, and we could tell he was worried about what it said.

"Wait a minute. Are you saying that she was planning on killing you?" I pried. "Does it actually say that in the journal?"

"No way, it couldn't. I hate to say it, but Marilyn was too smart to plan it out in writing," said Sally. Her face had been frozen in disbelief since we started talking about it. Which was kind of strange because I was usually the one to give people the benefit of the doubt.

"No, it doesn't say, 'I am going to kill Arden', but the outline, which she considered a comedy, is about a woman who tragically loses her husband in an accident involving an alligator at the Creole Nature Trail," Arden explained. "But I don't find it all that funny."

"A comedy. I really don't find it all that funny either. And you know, I keep not wanting to hate her, but that's not working out for me," I said. And then it hit me. The dream. This is what Carrie was talking about. She wasn't saying Arden was gonna die. I had to use my brain and put the song with the situation. Can't you see? Yeah, now I can! "Oh, my God, Arden. Carrie knew."

"What are you talking about?" he asked. "Explain yourself."

"I had a Carrie dream. And this is what she was trying to tell me. God, this is weird." Stewart was smiling at me, now. He knew I was okay because I had figured out what Carrie was trying to say. Trosclair looked a little confused.

"What song was playing?" asked Sally.

"Marshall Tucker Band, *Can't You See*," I said matter-of-factly, like I had it figured out from the get go. And then I told them the whole dream, the roses, the song, and as hard as it was to say out loud, seeing Arden's name on the plaque.

"Eerie," said Sally.

"Yeah, she woke up screaming. It wasn't pleasant," said Stewart.

"That Carrie. Always with the covert messages. But I'm glad she comes to you. I would have fallen out of the bed and died on the floor if I'd have had that dream," Arden said with a low chuckle. We all sat there quiet for a moment and then Trosclair spoke again.

"Well, Arden, you are right about one thing. This doesn't do anything to clear you with the police," he said. We could tell that he still didn't understand what had just transpired at the table. It was easier for him to just move on. "If anything, it makes you look like you have more of a motive. They could say that you knew about the plot and so you went after her first. What else was in her stuff?"

"Not much. Marilyn wasn't a sentimental kind of girl. Everything was garbage to her," said Arden.

"We need that box," said Stewart.

"But there's really nothing else in it."

"Stewart's right," said Trosclair. "Did you go through the whole thing?"

"Not every scrap of paper. What I found made me mad so I threw all the rest of her crap back in the box and shoved it in the closet."

"Stewart, go get the box," I said. "Go get it now."

Stewart got up from the table and headed toward the kitchen and out the back door. I heard him start the Jeep and pull out of the driveway.

"Okay, now that that is out of the way, what, pray tell, can I be accused of next?" Arden asked.

"Honey, don't be that way," said Sally.

"Dammit, I'm tired of being nice about Marilyn. Let Arden be mad, he deserves it." I really was exasperated as far as this whole thing went. "Hopefully this whole thing will be over soon. Trosclair, I mean Jules, did you listen to that tape? It clears Arden, you know it does."

"When can we throw it in their face?" asked Arden.

"Reign in your horses, Arden. This guy can't say one way or another that he didn't see you push her," said Jules.

"He saw Arden standing there after Marilyn bent down. Arden never made a move. How can you say that this guy didn't see that?" Sally asked. She was annoyed, I could tell.

"Calm down, Sal. Okay Jules, how does this work?" I asked.

"Well, they can say that he saw what he wanted to see, or that y'all bribed him to say what he said. The prosecution can come up with all kinds of theories to create reasonable doubt, that's their job."

"But this guy is fucking military. He has just as much to lose by lying. You need to put this in front of a judge," said Sally crossly.

"And I will. But I don't want you to get your hopes up."

"Fine."

"I'm sick of this topic," said Arden.

"It's making me want to vomit," I added. "What did you find out at the bank?"

"Prepare yourself for this, Arden," warned Jules.

"Since we all now know that she was a trashy whore, my guess would be that she was sleeping with the bank guy, right." Arden was almost always right about these things.

"Good guess."

"Slut."

"Nevers, really."

"Well, what else am I supposed to say? 'Poor Sweet Marilyn' is not something you'll hear fall from these lips." Jules explained that Marilyn had accomplished only so much online, but in order to make the huge transfers; she needed to be on the inside.

"So she made herself a friend," he said.

"And I know just how friendly she can be. This is gross," said Arden.

"Honey, if you want us to leave the room, we will," I told him.

"Why? I'll just have to drag through it again later when I tell y'all. No, stay and listen. Maybe there will be some entertainment value."

"According to this Elliot, she comes in one day; all dolled up and tells him she is a signer on the account and that she wants to move $500,000. And he's nervous. And without going into much detail, she apparently calmed his nerves...a couple of times," Jules explains.

"Oh, my gross. In the bank?" asks Sally.

"At least once in the bank that we know of."

"Isn't this a Janet Jackson song?" asked Arden. Miss Jackson, if you're nasty. For sure. And then Sally and I cracked up. We couldn't contain ourselves, and it felt good. And then Arden started in with his big cackle. Lord only knows what Jules Trosclair was thinking, but he let us laugh. He let us laugh long and hard; and he smiled while it was going on.

Stewart Speaks

I live in a crazy house, full of crazy people. That was all I could think of as I pulled out of the driveway and headed towards Arden's house. And the scariest part of all this is the fact that I love all those crazy people. I just hate what they are going through. It has been a rough week or so, and I've been trying to help, but most of the time that means staying out of the way. I was glad to have a job today. Because here's the thing: I know that Arden didn't have anything to do with all of this. And even though he is my friend, it is the toll it's taking on my wife that worries me.

Living the life I used to live, it never occurred to me that I would find someone like Nevers. Sure, she's a little neurotic, but that has gotten better over the last year or so. Actually, it started the night I proposed. She seemed to calm down after that. And once Arden came back to Lake Charles, all the pieces fell into place. But I knew that the peace wouldn't last forever. Good or bad, my wife and her friends have a knack for stirring things up. And trouble seems to find them, which doesn't make for a great gumbo, as Sally would say. And I have to agree.

It's like they live their life on the water and most of the time that water is calm. But eventually the waves start up. Sometimes Nevers, and Arden, and Sally make the waves, and sometimes outside forces step in and there is nothing anyone around them can do but ride it out. So that's what I'm doing. Riding out the storm.

I had just turned on some Shakira, which Nevers makes fun of me for, when my cell phone started to vibrate. The number was one I recognized and I hoped there was good news on the other end of the line.

"Lyle. Tell me something good," I said when I opened the phone. Lyle had worked for my family for years, and when my Grandmother and my cousin Muffy both died within days of each other, I sold him the business. I wanted out, and he was the one person I knew would do right by me and my Grandmother.

"I think my guys got what you were looking for. Listen to this. At the age of nineteen, one Marilyn Mercer, nee Simone, posed nude for a college boyfriend who was aspiring to be a photographer. They are nice, *nice* shots (leave it to Lyle), and up until about a year ago had been kept in a box in this guys basement."

"Oh, shit. Graphic?"

"Pretty much."

"So he drags them out so he can blackmail her?"

"No, that's the thing. She calls him out of the blue and says she wants them. He's married now, with kids. But he is in business for himself and figures the money wouldn't hurt. The guy's legit. He wasn't trying to ruin her life. She started it."

"Wow. So she calls him and offers money, but she doesn't have that kind of dough on hand so she steals Arden's. Is that how this is playing out?"

"From what I can gather. The people at the studio said the way the deal went down she got some money up front and then optioned to take fifty percent of the box office, so she didn't have much on hand. The only thing this Bob guy is guilty of is setting a high price, but when he finds out she's sold a screenplay he figures she's got it." I don't even bother to ask Lyle how he got the information from the studio; he's got more connections than a box of *Legos*.

"Will this guy sign a statement?"

"It's done and should be at your house in Lake Charles today. And don't worry about negatives or anything; my guys took care of that."

"Lyle, what would I do without you?"

"I don't know, kid. Oh, and listen. We found the foster parents. They did their best but they say Marilyn was wild; sleeping around and taking older men for their money starting when she turned fifteen. They reported it so they wouldn't get in trouble, and when she moved out at seventeen they let her go. I mean really, they weren't going to fight her. She had some sugar daddy in the Village, went to live with him."

"Good God. Okay Lyle. I owe you. When are you coming down so we can go fishing?"

"Soon, soon. Look, give my love to Nevers and tell Arden to hang in there. I'll talk to you soon."

When I hung up with Lyle, I was elated. We had proof that Marilyn was trash. And I hate to say that, but when it comes down to my friend going to jail for something he didn't do or smearing the name of his dead wife, I'll take smearing any day. I got to Arden's house and went to retrieve the box. It was easy enough to find because it was probably the only plastic thing in the house. Arden must have hated that, even though it was in the closet. And I know he missed being at home, but it needed a good overhaul before he came back. I thought about calling the Merry Maids, but Trosclair had said the cops may still want to go through it, so I put that idea on the back burner.

I called Nevers to let her know that I got the box, and told her I was going to check things at the shop. She told me she loved me (which still got me going, a year later) and said she was going to take a nap. I would like to have been able to lie down with her and I told her so. "But you wouldn't let me sleep," she said. And she was probably right. We'd been through so much in the brief time that we had been married, that sex had become scarce. But that was okay. Nevers was fun to tease, and as long as she let me do that, things were good.

I headed downtown to RPM's, and parked across the street in a private lot, which I shouldn't have been parking in, but I was in too good a mood to care. I hadn't said anything to Nevers, because I wanted to surprise all of them when I got back to the house. Going to RPM's was really just a way of killing time until the documents from Lyle arrived. Plus, I loved the store. It reeked of my wife and that put me in a good mood. There was a good flow of business going on and I found Kiki behind the counter talking Marvin Gaye with some college guy. She looked involved so I waved and went to find Wes.

"Praise, God," he said when he saw me, "I've been trying all morning to get this shit in order." He waved his arms referring to the piles of paper covering the desk. "But your wife, man, she's got some kind of system that I cannot understand."

"Don't sweat it, Wes. Listen, can you keep a secret? I got some information today and I want to know if it sounds as good as I think it does."

"This about that Arden stuff? Cause I almost had to take out some frat boy last night, you know, represent. He was talking some shit about my boy." I loved it when Wes took on his "homie" persona. He had a couple different ones, but this one and the bad martial arts movie accent were my favorites.

"Yeah, but I think what I found out this morning is gonna help." And I proceeded to tell him the story, in full detail.

"I get to see the pictures, right?"

"We'll see," I said laughing. Wes' exuberance as a young male always amazed me.

"And I can tell Kiki, right?" Wes was brimming over with excitement.

"Yeah, but it goes no further. So you think this will help?" I asked.

"Dirty pictures always get the job done."

"What dirty pictures?" asked Kiki from the doorway. "I swear I leave this delinquent alone for five minutes and he's back here talking shit to you. Don't believe a word he says, Stewart."

"Stewart brought it up. I just asked if I could get a glimpse."

"It's true," I said.

"What are you doing with dirty pictures? Unless they are of Nevers. Ooohhh, are they of Nevers? I knew that girl had some trashy in her," Kiki said with a laugh.

"Look, I gotta get out of here. Wes, you explain." And with that I gathered up some of the paper work that had to be done and headed out the front of the shop. When I walked outside I noticed movement in a car parked a couple of spaces down from mine. And then I saw Eva get out. I didn't recognize the car, but the guy I knew. He'd been to my house. It was Detective Owens.

"Fancy meeting you here," I said, leaning up against the hood of the Jeep nonchalantly.

"God, you've been hanging around Nevers too long. Don't give me any shit today, I can't take it," she said.

"What's going on?"

"This quest of Ezra's. He thinks he knows why Arden is being prosecuted so vigorously, but it all sounds simple to me. I'm not saying that Ezra is wrong, but there is no way that it could be this easy."

"I'm on my way to the house. Trosclair is there with everybody; we could see what he thinks." I knew Eva needed a sounding board, just like I had. Things were getting good again; turning in our favor I could feel it. And I for one was glad. I was ready to have some fun; it had already been a hard year. "Could I tempt you with some scandalous pictures?" I asked.

"Depends on who they're of," Eva said.

"Don't worry about it. They're gonna be good."

We got in the Jeep and Eva immediately started trying to justify being in the car with Detective Owens. She explained that they were trying to keep in quiet, or on the down low, as Kiki would say, but they really liked each other. She went on to say that they really felt they had something, and that they hated sneaking around, but they just couldn't wait until the investigation was over. I told her I thought they were in love and she laughed. But then she got quiet, and a scared look came over her face, and she said, "Oh, shit, Stewart. I think you might be right." And then I started laughing.

When we arrived at the house Eva went in to find everybody, while I got the box. I took the box and put it under a work bench in the garage. I didn't really think that anyone would come looking for it, but I also didn't want to take any chances. When I walked in, Sally told me I had some delivery on the table in the small foyer. "Where's my wife?" She's still asleep, I was told. Sally and Arden were camped out in the den watching *Gone with the Wind*. "Askin' ain't gettin'," said someone from the den. Trosclair was at the computer.

"Hope you don't mind," he said. "It's much more comfortable here than in that hotel room." I told him to make himself at home, and I meant it. Jules is a good guy. I headed to the foyer to get the package, and then I made my way to the bedroom to see my wife.

"Hey beautiful," I said moving the hair away from her eyes. "I think I got some good news."

"Well that's nice to hear. Now quit kissing my neck. What's the good news?"

So I told her the story, the whole thing. The conversation with Lyle and what he'd found out. "You are lying," she said; a phrase that covered a lot of ground as far as my wife and her friends were concerned. I told her I wasn't, the stock reply, but that I was worried about how Arden would take the news. Nevers said that after this morning Arden really couldn't care less. He was tired of being blamed for all this shit. Especially when it turns out that Marilyn was the cad. "Well, then he's gonna love this," I said. And so we went to gather everybody for a little show and tell.

And that's pretty much the way it is around here. Nevers is right when she says the good always comes with the bad. Meeting her was the best thing that ever happened to me, and then I lost my Grandmother. But then Nevers said she'd marry me, and then came her cancer. It's like movie stars dying in threes, you just can't avoid it. And so I am looking forward to all of this being over soon, because as my mother-in-law would say, "this too shall pass." I'm not sure if I married into cliché heaven, or if it's the same way all over the South. But no matter what happens, good or bad, there's a saying for it.

I was still a little worried about how the pictures would affect Arden. I know that I wouldn't want to see photos of Nevers like that. And before you think I'm a big prude, let me just say that, yes, nude pictures of my wife would be nice...you know, something tasteful. But the pictures of Marilyn were far from tasteful. To be frank they are down-right nasty. Not that I'd ever say that to Arden. But Arden is a smart guy. And I don't think he'll consider them tasteful either.

Jules Trosclair

My very first case involved a woman named Vivian
Vanderkellan-Woods. I was working for a big,
prestigious firm out of New Orleans, and they figured a
divorce would be easy for me to handle. How wrong
they were. Vivian, as she asked me to call her, had
decided to take her husband for everything he was
worth, deciding that the generous five million offer he
made was too little. But the entire case was crazy.
Vivian accused her husband of cheating on her with the
Portuguese maid. Mr. Woods accused Vivian of
cheating on him with the pool boy. And it all went
downhill from there. Of course no one had any serious
proof of anything, and their friends could only speculate.

"Well, there was this one day. I ran into Miles (the
husband) at Tiffany's and he was purchasing this
fabulous tennis bracelet that never made it onto Vivian's
wrist. So where do you think it went? Straight to that
trashy maid, that's where." This was the kind of thing I
got no matter who I asked. No one could ever prove that
Miles gave the bracelet to the maid, just as no one could
ever prove that Vivian had purchased a whole new
wardrobe for the pool boy, which reportedly included
Speedos and silk suits. The case dragged on for months,
with a judge finally deciding the outcome, because
neither myself, nor the attorney for Mr. Woods could
ever get them to agree on anything. Vivian ended up
with the house, though, which meant she kept the pool
boy.

The Arden Mercer case was starting to feel the same
way to me. We had so much information, and I wasn't
sure what any of it was going to get us. And I had a
week to sort it out. We had the missing money,
transferred by the deceased, who also slept with the

bank employee, we had the eyewitness testimony from an Air Force Tech Sergeant saying that he and his wife didn't see Arden push his wife; we had a screenplay written by the deceased detailing the murder of a husband by his wife at the Creole Nature Trail. We had too much shit. And then Stewart came back to the house with Eva and they had even more. Even though it was only one o'clock in the afternoon, I poured myself a scotch. And I wasn't the only one.

As we gathered around the dining room table, which had become Mercer Trial Central, I noticed that Arden and Stewart had cracked open a couple of Red Stripes, and Eva was joining me with scotch. Nevers and Sally were sipping Cokes. We were a multifarious group, the six of us. With one common goal: to figure out what the hell was going on. And with information coming at us from all sides, it was like standing in the middle of a blizzard. You'd like to shield your eyes, but then you can't see what's going to hit you in the face.

"So, who goes first?" I asked.

"I'll go," said Stewart, pulling out an envelope. "I spoke with Lyle Gugino this morning. As you all know, I had him looking into Marilyn's past. He found the foster parents. Here is their statement." And he passed a sheaf of papers around the table. We all watched for Arden's reaction when he read it. We got a belly laugh.

"I must be slipping," he said. "I used to be able to spot tacky at a mile away. Never thought I'd be a sugar daddy, though."

"You might want to rethink that adjective when you see this. She was trying to make these go away, that's what the money was for. But she never got the chance to transfer it to this Bob guy," said Stewart.

"Holy shit," said Sally. "Um, there's her…and, whoa. Boy, here's an interesting shot." For once in her life Sally had no words as she turned the pictures this way and that.

"Full cooch," said Arden. "It figures."

"You know, there are some things about people that you don't ever need to know. The fact that she shaved a heart there, well, I think I could have gone my whole life without knowing that and I would have been okay," said Nevers.

"It was a star before she, you know…" said Arden.

"Didn't need to know that either," said Eva. And they all started laughing. I wanted to, but I figured, as Arden's attorney, I should maintain some respectability. But that was the thing about this group, they swallowed everything with humor.

"Maybe I could sell them to Hugh and get some of my money back," said Arden.

"Nope, this is strictly Larry Flint territory," said Nevers. And they all cracked up again.

"Alright, back to business. Could someone please put those back in the envelope?" I asked.

"Yeah, I haven't had lunch yet," said Sally. More laughter.

"What did you find out, Eva?" I pressed. I wanted to get things moving so I could sort all this crap out and decide what to do with it.

"Well, I didn't find it, but here's the deal. Arden, I don't know if you know this, but your Mama dated Sheriff Arceneaux in high school," said Eva.

"Okay, y'all already made me nauseous once today," said Arden.

"It's true, it was their senior year. But she was smart enough to break up with him. The only problem is that she broke up with him right before a huge football game. And during that football game he took a beating. So he ends up blowing out his knee and just like that his football career was over. He blames her for the whole thing. And Ezra, I mean Detective Owens, thinks that that is the whole reason he brought charges against you in the first place," she explained.

"Is this really possible?" asked Sally.

"Well, Ezra thinks it is, but he's taken it as far as he can. Any more digging will get him in a lot of trouble."

"Well, I know one way we can find out," said Arden. "Nevers, hand me the phone." And Arden called France, woke up his Mama and finally told her everything that was going on. While they were talking, Sally went to get Jackson so she could feed him, and Nevers followed them into the kitchen.

"So who is this Lyle Gugino guy?" I asked Stewart, who laughed in response.

"He's the guy who is going to come fishing with us when this is all over. I'll let him tell you the rest when he gets here," said Stewart. Arden had left the table and was pacing around the den at this point. We heard a lot of "Yes, Ma'am" which made us laugh. Except for Eva, who was looking a little down.

"What's up, honey?" Stewart asked her.

"I can't imagine how Arden is feeling. I mean, I am so ready for all of this to be over. The last week or so has felt like a year, you know what I mean?"

"I see what you're screaming," said Nevers coming back into the dining room. She was carrying a drink this time. And then Sally poked her head in the doorway to let everyone know she and Jackson were heading home.

"Can you give me a ride?" asked Eva.

"Sure. Nevers, please call and let me know what's going on later," Sally requested.

And then they were gone. I sat at that table looking at all the accumulated paper and wondering where to go from here. Nevers was resting her head on Stewart's shoulder and I could tell that all of this was taking a toll on her. I noticed that she hadn't even bothered to put her wig on since they'd gotten back from Tucson, and she looked like a little pixie, small and scared. I also took note of the fact that as soon as Arden walked back into the room the look of fear was replaced by a look of hope. Never let them see you down.

"Well, she's on her way home," Arden said, referring to his Mama.

"Poor thing," said Nevers. "I hate to see her making the trip. She hasn't had much of a turn-around."

"She said it was okay. Apparently she got in trouble for going to the Louvre. You know my Mama."

"So, Jules, where do we go from here?" asked Stewart.

"I'm going to call ADA Whitman and set up a meeting in the morning. I'm going to bring all this information with me," I said waving my hands over the mounds of paper on the table, "and we'll see what they have to say. I can't see him wanting to pursue this a whole lot longer, but you never know. So my advice to you, Arden is to get some rest now. Even if they drop the charges, it could still get a little crazy. One of my assistants informed me this morning that a couple of newspapers picked up the story."

"Oh, great. Not only am I some kind of miscreant in my hometown, now it's going nationwide."

"What newspapers?" asked Nevers.

"Pretty much all the big ones. Once the AP picked it up, that was it. You're famous to begin with. People are eating it up." It wasn't really what we needed, but we couldn't stop it.

"I guess it was a good thing that you called your Mama. If she'd had to read about it in the Paris papers, she'd have flown home just to kick your ass," Nevers told Arden.

"You're right. She would have been bitter."

The Warrant to Search

When Jules left, we decided that dinner was in order, being that we'd kind of put off lunch and had started drinking. Stewart went to call Dagastino's, because they delivered, but before he could pick up the phone, it rang. Arden and I sat quiet and tried to figure out what was going on from the "yeahs" and "uh-huh's" we were hearing. "That was Jules," said Stewart. "We have to go to Arden's house. They've issued a search warrant." So we piled into Stewart's Jeep, and headed over there. The scene was amazing; I think there were six patrol cars, lining the street. We spotted Jules standing in the driveway, holding the search warrant in his had, a grim look on his face. It was his game face, so I knew that things were serious.

"It's a good damn thing you came to get the box this morning," I told Stewart as we got out of the car.

"Yeah, but now there's nothing personal in the house belonging to her," said Arden. "That could look bad."

"She has things in the house. Make-up, perfume, clothes. If they ask, you just tell them she didn't bring anything with her when he moved in," I said.

"So, you want me to lie?"

"It's not like you've never done it before."

"Well, yeah, but not to the cops."

"Y'all shut-up, Jules wants us over there," said Stewart, leading us across the street to the driveway. "How bad does it look?" he asked Jules.

"I don't think they even know what they're looking for," said Jules. "And since the box is gone, well, they won't find anything. Right Arden?"

"No, but I'm a little worried about that box."

"Don't be. The journal was the thing to worry about, and that's not in the box. And they have no reason at all to search the Wainwright house, so just be cool."

So we stood there in the driveway. I could tell things were tense because Stewart bummed a smoke from me and the last time I saw him smoke was when his Grandmother died. Sally said that he smoked while I was in surgery, but I didn't witness that. One of Arden's neighbors came over to say hello. He shook Arden's hand and said they (his neighbors) were all hoping for the best. When the guy left, Arden said he was full of shit. We stood there a few minutes longer. Arden could have gone in the house, but didn't see a need to until we saw the local news van coming down the street.

"What the fuck is all this?" he asked.

"Nevers, walk Arden to the backyard, please," Jules requested calmly.

"Why do I have to go to the backyard? This is my house, and I really don't want them here," said Arden.

"You need to go to the backyard because if you are not available for comment, they won't hang around. Look, you hired me to represent you. Let me do my job."

"Y'all go. I'll stay with Jules and report back," said Stewart. So Arden and I fled to the backyard, but once there, we climbed through overgrown azalea bushes to get behind the fence so we could peer through the slats. It was totally juvenile, but so were we. And we weren't going to miss a thing.

"Can you believe this?" he asked.

"The search or being in the bushes?" I asked him.

"Really, Nevers. What is going on?"

"You got stuck in a bad place, Arden. But if we have to grease you up like a pig to get you out of it, we will."

"It feels like a freak show."

"Maybe they won't even air it. They won't get much out of Jules."

And apparently they didn't. The cheesy blond girl from the evening news got out, cameraman following closely behind. She was wearing an ill-fitting mauve suit and smiling broadly when she approached Jules, but he didn't have much to say. And whatever he did tell her must have pissed her off because she turned around and stomped off rather quickly, her mules slapping on the driveway. This sent Arden and I into peals of laughter which made her look over her shoulder. But we quickly stifled ourselves. It wouldn't do Arden any good for the news hounds or the cops to hear us laughing, especially if we had to explain why we were laughing.

Arden and I waited until the news van was gone and then we made our way out of the bushes, brushing leaves out of hair and off our clothes, and walked back to the driveway. Stewart had the look on his face that said: *Don't ask now, I'll tell you later.* We stood there a few more minutes before seeing a cop come out the back door with a brown paper bag in his hand. I could tell Arden was a little shaken up, but we knew we got the most damaging thing out of the house, so it left us puzzled. A few more minutes and a couple more cops passed before Sheriff Arceneaux himself came out. In a gesture of southern manners, he shook Jules' hand and said they were through. Jules thanked him and we turned, the four of us, in what seemed like a choreographed move, toward the back door; Arden went in first.

"It doesn't look like I thought it would," he said.

"What do you mean?" asked Jules.

"Well, on the cop shows on TV the place is always torn up. Drawers open, stuffing coming out of the sofa," he explained.

"Arden, I told you this was for show. They knew they weren't going to find anything. It wasn't like you wrote down how you were going to do it and left it taped to the fridge," said Jules.

"Yeah, that was Marilyn, except for the fridge part," I said.

"So, is anything missing?" asked Stewart. Arden wasn't sure so he asked me to walk through the house with him. I'd spent enough time at Arden's to know the contents pretty well. I'd lived with him for awhile after a fire burned down my original business and attached apartment. I decided after that to always have my home at least a mile away from my workplace. And when I talk about all that we've been through already, this is the kind of thing I'm referring to. I mean, writing the book was a big deal for us, we went on national television, we did book signings all over the country, and we made lots of money. But we also experienced the loss of my home and business, the death of Stewart's cousin Muffy, and the all important falling out between Arden and me. We of course had some good times; Stewart and I getting married, Sally having Jackson. But it wasn't long before the shit hit the fan again.

And that is the way it is with us. We have those good times, and then, BAM, here come the bad. There was the wedding, and the glorious honeymoon, and then, look out, Nevers is down for the count with cancer growing on her ovaries and uterus. I mean, I was lucky that it was caught so early that it didn't spread, but still. It's always something. That's why it was so nice when baby Jackson came. He gave us all new life, the way only a baby can, and at the time it seemed like things might actually be looking up for Arden and Marilyn. Of course we never realized what a front Arden was putting up. I cringe when I think of what he was really going through. And it made me wonder what kind of person I really am, now that she was gone and I felt no remorse.

I think it's like when a parent loses a child in a violent, terrible way. No matter how decent they may be, I imagine that they would want the person responsible for the death of their child to pay. And so it is with Arden. If Marilyn wouldn't have died, and we had found out all the things she'd done, and most importantly, what she'd been planning to do, I'd have taken her out myself. And trust me, no one would have found her body. And even though I usually feel guilty for almost everything in my life, I don't think I would have felt it when it came to dealing with Marilyn.

With all the information we'd gotten today, I figured Marilyn for crazy. I mean, who starts taking old men for their money before they're even legal. And poses for nasty (and they are nasty) pictures and then has sex with a bank employee so she can steal money from her husband to try to get the pictures back. And, biggest of all, plots to kill their husband in a horrific way. See, the deal is that Marilyn never knew Arden. If she did, she would have known that she could have asked him for the money and he would have given it to her. Despite everything, Arden loved her. And I know that that is why he is struggling now; calling her names and putting her down. It's easier for him this way. It's easier for all of us. And I think, in a strange way, it was easier for Marilyn to do things in her way, the way she'd been doing them all her life. Sleep with somebody, get the pictures back, and then kill Arden. She'd have all her ducks in a row. She'd have her life back.

God, maybe that's the only reason she married Arden at all. Maybe she just wanted the money to get the pictures back. And maybe she planned to kill him all along. Even if she didn't write the screenplay, she could have sold the story of her husband being mauled to death by an alligator to one of her L.A. connections. If packaged properly with, you know, some crotch-less panties and a push-up bra, she could have made a mint.

God only knows what would have happened. And that is why I'm glad she's out of our lives. Now if we could get this whole mess dismissed, I'd feel a lot better. And it would take a while, but Arden would get back to his old self. Really, I don't think anybody in town thought that he was responsible. Or maybe it was because she was an outsider; had she been a local it might have been different. But Marilyn was "that New York City girl who married Arden Mercer."

Nevers

"Goddammit, they took my cowboy boots," yelled Arden from the back of the house. Stewart immediately looked at me and my face turned red.

"I'll explain later," I said to Jules, when he caught the exchange between Stewart and me. And then I walked to the back bedroom to see Arden.

"Dammit, Nevers, they took my boots."

"I don't think so honey. There's no way they could have been in that bag they carried out. Maybe they are at my house, or your Mama's." It was important for me to throw him off as far as the boots were concerned because at that moment they were at Exotic Custom Boots and Shoes in Houston being copied for a new pair.

"No, I remember them being here that morning because I contemplated wearing a jean, but I knew it was gonna get too hot."

"Well then, I'll call the Sheriff's office when we get home and try to find out what's going on. What else did they take?"

"Her make-up and perfume and stuff like that," he said.

"Well that doesn't make a whole lot of sense. How can that be used against you?"

"Who knows? I tell you Nevers, this whole thing is a fuckery."

"I'm with you on that one. Come on, let's go home. We'll get something to eat on the way, and later we can watch *Gentlemen Prefer Blondes*, and you and Stewart can throw things at me for singing too loud."

We walked back through the house and found Stewart and Jules sitting at the little table in the kitchen, drinking Cokes from the fridge. Stewart was smoking another cigarette. Jules reminded Arden again that this was all for show. "I'm going to talk to the judge in the morning. It's obvious they didn't find anything today, and they need to let this go," he said. And with that we headed out the door. Jules headed back to the hotel to work, even though we told him he could come back to the house because we knew he was more comfortable there.

But I think Jules needed to be away from us. Arden and I, well, we're known for being able to drain every last bit of energy from a person's body. Stewart always says it's a good thing, that he feels cleansed every morning, ready to start over. God, I love that man. So we headed back to The Drive, stopping at Dagastino's for pizza on the way. Don't ask me why, but when we got pizza's I ordered extras because you just never know. And it was a good thing, because when we got back to the house Kiki and Wes were sitting on the front porch swing. They were sipping to-go margaritas from Casa, and laughing. They looked so at ease, and I was a little jealous. I wanted that feeling back in my life.

"Hey, y'all," I called out, "what's going on?"

"Aw, you know how we roll," said Wes, which made Kiki laugh even harder.

"How many of those have y'all had?" I asked.

"One too many, I think," said Kiki, holding out her Styrofoam cup as an offering.

"She's been teaching me slang," said Wes.

"Yeah, I could tell. Come on in, I got a bunch of pizza." See, I told you, always expect the unexpected. And as far as I was concerned, Kiki and Wes were my kids; the least I could do was feed them. They did so much for me.

"Where y'all been?" asked Wes. Even after the margarita's he sounded worried.

"At my house," said Arden. "The cops were there with a search warrant."

"No way," said Wes in disbelief. This whole thing with Arden was so silly to Wes and Kiki that they kept waiting for a punch line. Always optimistic, my faithful employees, that's why I loved them. After my surgery, they'd come over and make me laugh so hard I thought my stitches were gonna pop.

"They didn't find anything," said Stewart. "Jules says it was just for show. So far they don't have anything concrete, their case is all circumstantial. And I don't think that Whitman is fool enough to go to court with what Arceneaux brings him. No matter how bad he wants to."

"All he has is the missing money, and that's not enough. Especially when they find out why she took it," said Arden.

"Wait, y'all found out what was going on with the money?" asked Kiki.

"I forgot to tell her that part. I just blabbed about the *Hustler*-esque pictures," said Wes invoking a little Arden by using the word 'blab'.

"Come on, let's eat and we'll tell y'all everything," I said.

We walked in the house and Arden brought the pizzas to the dining room. Stewart went and grabbed a bunch of Abita from the fridge while I walked around opening windows. It was cool outside and I wanted to take advantage of it. Stewart and I had replaced all the old windows when we bought the house and the new ones had the built in screens which were very convenient. I really did love my house. And even though I knew it was under rotten circumstances, I loved having Arden here; I loved having people in my house. And everyone came to our house. It was kind of like my Mama's house when we were younger. Maybe it was the location. I mean, the lake wasn't the most beautiful lake in the world, but it was a body of water right outside our front door.

South Lake Charles? Well, there's nothing wrong with it. I was just born and raised downtown. It's what I know. The strip malls and restaurants going up south of town scared me. They made Lake Charles look like any other city in the country. I liked being where I was because everything was familiar. We had Maryann's, OB's, the Civic Center, Crystal's. When we were little we had Abe's and Joseph's Pizza, and The Wizard, which was Mae Mae's now, but that doesn't stop us from calling it The Wizard. We used to ride our bikes to The Racquet Club on hot summer days, and I think it is sad because you don't see kids doing that anymore. I understand progress, I do, but that doesn't mean it can't irk me. And I hated that Sally lived south of town, but I did get to pick on her because of it.

I realized then that I needed to call her, but I had to have food first. So we all sat down at the table and ate, drinking cold Abita Turbo Dog, and we told Kiki and Wes all the latest. There was a lot of laughter, of course. And there is nothing better than a bunch of friends sitting around a table laughing. Especially when things are less than perfect. We decided to relocate to the den when everyone was full. Stewart grabbed everyone a new beer, and we all claimed our spots in front of the TV. But when Kiki and Wes found out we were going to watch *Gentlemen Prefer Blondes* they issued a veto. "We've all seen it too many times," said Wes. And I figured if he said it, it was probably time to give it a rest. Kiki and Wes talked us into watching *Top Chef* on *Bravo*.

Sally

When Nevers called me the next morning, I felt a glimmer of hope. It sounds crazy, but I was the one with the legal mind, and I knew that if they didn't find anything in the house then they really were grasping for straws. I had called Trosclair myself and discussed all this with him. He felt the same way, but reminded me how small town justice works. I wondered if they, the cops or the prosecutor, had something they weren't sharing. Jules hadn't asked for anything yet, because he felt like we had enough to get Arden off, but I'm always one for killing the cat.

I asked Jules if it was okay to involve his intern Gretchen in a little detective work and he gave me the go ahead. I also needed to call Detective Owens. I knew that he'd already put himself in a precarious situation regarding this case, but I needed one more favor, and he was my inside guy. Here's the thing that had been keeping me awake at night. Arden had Marilyn's bracelet. It had come off in his hand when he tried to pull her out of the jaws of…well, you know. Anyway. What I couldn't figure out was this: Marilyn never went anywhere without her cheesy Louis Vuitton wristlet. Where was that? Of course my first call was to Arden to see if he knew.

"God, Sally, I hadn't even thought of that. It must have gone in the water with her," he said.

"Are you sure she had it with her on the trail?" He didn't even have to think about it.

"Yes. Because I remember telling her it was stupid. You know, carrying that damn bag. Like there was somewhere to buy refreshments or cocktails on the Creole Nature Trail. She said she didn't want to leave it in the car because it might get stolen. I gave up. I didn't even try to explain that people in Hackberry could give a fuck about a Louis Vuitton wristlet. The morning was going so well that I didn't want to fan the flames. Why is this important?"

"It might not be," I said. "But what if it didn't go in the water? Let's face it; after she went in, I doubt you thought about looking for her purse. And if by chance it didn't go in, where is it? Actually, even if it did, they might have recovered it."

"But what is so important about her purse?"

"Who knows? But think about this…she didn't keep too much personal stuff at the house, maybe she had something in that damn purse that would shed some light on what went down."

"Well, get to work, Nancy Drew. See what you can find," he said.

I called Gretchen, who agreed to help. Which was good because she actually worked for Jules Trosclair, I didn't. And then I called Detective Owens. I called his cell phone. Eva was reluctant to give me the number, but she knew I wouldn't ask if it wasn't important. And I was not about to call the Sheriff's Department directly. I gotta give it to the guy, he was pleasant, though a little confused. "I'll call down to the evidence room and let them know you're coming," he said.

"I wish you wouldn't. I know they hate surprises, but what if they alert someone?"

"Sally, it isn't as archaic as all that."

"But how do you know? Arceneaux could have someone working down there."

"Okay, I won't call. But can I ask what it is you're looking for?"

"Just a piece of the puzzle that might not even be there."

I brought Jackson to Nevers. She was always trying to get me to do things so she could baby sit, and here was her chance. He didn't even cry when I left. Of course he had three grown-ups hanging on his every "coo"; three grown-ups who were spending the day on pins and needles, waiting for some good news. Part of me wanted to be there, but another part of me was just sure that we were missing something. So I left my baby in the best hands, hands which would spoil him rotten, and drove over to get Gretchen. I explained my theory in the car on the way to the Sheriff's Department. I could tell she didn't have much hope. "Even if it's there," she said, "there's no guarantee that they haven't taken things out of it."

But it wasn't there. And I believed the guy who told us. He'd gone to high school with us and was a good guy. He even told us, cryptically that he didn't believe anything that was being said about Arden. "Dude helped me get through Algebra II my sophomore year. Woulda failed it if it wasn't for Arden." It wasn't what I considered to be a life-changing event, but this guy went on to explain that had he failed it would have meant no football, and at this point we all understood how important football was. Apparently, his Algebra grades got him into LSU. We thanked him and headed out to the car. We sat there for a long time without talking.

I could tell Gretchen as trying to figure out where the purse was. Had it not gone into the water it would have been picked up at the scene. If it did go in the water, they would have recovered it when the dragged the water. They did that very thoroughly, I knew because they were looking for anything that would point the finger at Arden. And it couldn't have been left in the alligator, or could it? "Feel like taking a little drive with me?" I asked Gretchen. "I'm game," she said, and I laughed and laughed. If she only knew. Gretchen had never been down to Hackberry before, but she thought it was beautiful. I knew she was good people right then and there. I asked her where she was from.

"Right over in Jennings. I graduated from USL, you know, before they changed the name," she explained.

"Why law school? And why the investigative work?" I asked.

"My Dad worked for the plants."

"Killed or Cancer?"

"Killed. And of course we got jackshit. It didn't bother me too much, but my Mama was devastated. I have three younger brothers and she had a hard time working and keeping them in line. I wanted to make sure that never happened to anyone else. I know it sounds cliché, but it's true. The investigative stuff just ended up being more satisfying than the law end of it. I liked finding out what people were up to behind closed doors. You'd be amazed."

"I doubt it. But I think your reasons are better than the ones most people have," I told her; and I meant it. Most people around here were only in law for the money. There are a few around town who do it for the right reasons, too few. I liked Gretchen, and I liked her priorities. The fact that she's beautiful would make some women uncomfortable, but Nevers and I had decided, with our aging wisdom, that it doesn't do you any good to be jealous. Besides, my boobs were way bigger than Gretchen's.

Gretchen didn't ask where we were going, but I think she knew. And if she did know, she wasn't prying about my knowledge of the location. It was better that no one knew why Nevers and I had been there the first time. We turned onto the drive that led to Mr. Trahan's property and Gretchen was amazed that someone actually lived out here. When we rounded the last curve and she saw the water she changed her mind. "It's pretty," she said, sounding amazed. I warned her to watch were she was walking when we got out of the car. Mr. Trahan had a dog, something that Nevers and I didn't realize the first time we'd been out here. It wasn't until we were at the main road that we realized that someone was carrying around evidence of said dog.

Mr. Trahan was sitting in an old rocking chair on his porch when we approached him. "Help ya?" he asked. I guess he didn't recognize me. That was actually a good thing though, because now Gretchen could take the lead. She had a legal reason to be there, I didn't. My reasons were so personal as to be desperate, and it was probably best if I didn't open my mouth. Of course I could have been mistaken. Gretchen explained why we were there, telling him in the simplest of terms that the purse that the deceased had been carrying was missing, and if he knew anything about it he should tell us, because if the cops came out it could get ugly.

"You work for that Mercer boy?" he asked Gretchen.

"Yes, sir I do," she replied cautiously. You had to be careful giving out info in a situation like this.

"Strange situation," he said. "But that boy didn't kill his wife."

"And you know this how?" I asked. I gotta admit I was worried about pressing him too hard, but he never said anything about all this when Nevers and I were out here the first time. Of course, we didn't ask, either.

"That woman, the one got killed; she had on too much perfume. Way I heard it she was trying to get close to them babies. Smell of her was still on that nest when I went back to get 'em."

"Her perfume?" Gretchen wondered aloud.

"Yep. Gators know shit when they smell it. That Mama thought her babies were in danger, that's why she done it. Didn't have nothing to do with that Mercer boy. If he'd a pushed her in that Mama gator woulda swum away from the smell of her," he said laughing at his own musings. I didn't know if any of this held water, but the local cops or the Wildlife and Fisheries guys could tell us.

"So what do you think happened to her purse?" I asked.

"I think if it was on her it ended up inside the gator," he replied matter-of-factly.

"Well..." said Gretchen.

"Oh, I got it, if that's what you're won'dren. Figured sooner or later somebody'd come looking for it. Guess I was right."

"Can we have it?" I asked.

"Whatcha give me for it?" Good, God, I thought. Nevers and I had already given this guy the boat that was tied to the little dock out back and a wad of cash. But I couldn't blame him. The money Nevers and I had given him could probably get him through a whole year; another five hundred dollars could get him even further.

"That's bribery, Mr. Trahan," said Gretchen.

"I got something you want. I call it business." I couldn't help it, I started laughing. Mr. Trahan smiled affectionately in my direction.

"How much?" I asked. Gretchen cut her eyes at me and I could tell she disapproved, but if I was paying for it she couldn't get in trouble. I only had two hundred on me but I told Mr. Trahan that I would bring him three more.

"You'll bring it by the end of the week?"

"Yes, sir, I will."

"I'll go get you the purse," he said, straining to get out of the rocker. I thought about offering my hand, but I knew old men like him and I knew he would have been offended. He reminded me of my Grandfather, you know the kind of man who doesn't want to get old because he doesn't want anybody having to wipe his behind for him.

"You shouldn't have done that," said Gretchen.

"No, you shouldn't have done it. I, on the other hand, am a private citizen. I can do what I want."

"Still. If this gets out, it could hurt us."

"I wouldn't worry about that," I said, knowing that Mr. Trahan wouldn't breathe a word of it. And I was right. After he brought us the purse, Gretchen put it in a big Ziploc bag and headed back to the car. I stood there a moment longer to say thank you and shake Mr. Trahan's hand. "Told you I wouldn't remember you," he said with a sly smile. I walked away laughing.

I also wasn't worried because I had the feeling that the Sheriff was up to something, and believe me, it was probably illegal, or if not illegal at least unethical. I thought about explaining it to Gretchen, but deep down inside I think she already knew that especially in the state of Louisiana, you had to fight fire with fire, even if that meant doing things you would normally find morally repulsive. Like viewing the pictures of Marilyn.

Gretchen would learn this lesson on her own if she stayed in the business she was in. It sounds like a bad movie plot, I know, but most of the time it just works that way. I, personally, have come to believe that the world is morally bankrupt. If it wasn't, there wouldn't be reality television.

Arden

I was trying hard not to think about how much I was going to owe Nevers and Sally for all they'd done. They would never ask for anything in return, but I would feel obligated to do something for the two of them. This was one of those times when a thank you note just wasn't enough. When Sally showed up on the front porch of The Drive with Marilyn's purse in her hand I almost fell over and died. I wanted to know where she got it, and then I thought better of it.

If she had to, Sally would have stuck her hand up that alligator's ass to get it, and the debt would have been unimaginable. We figured it was best to let Jules in on the action so Nevers went to give him a call. Nevermind that he had a meeting with the prosecutor and the judge in two hours, he was at the house in less than ten minutes. Of course we were paying him good money for just this kind of thing.

"Do I want to know where you got this?" Jules asked.

"Probably not," said Gretchen.

"There was nothing illegal about it. We couldn't steal it from the Sheriff Department's evidence room because they didn't have it. It was a business transaction," Sally explained. I heaved a sigh of relief. There was no felony involved.

"Well, let's have a look," said Jules, opening the Ziploc. He'd pulled on a pair of latex gloves before he started handling it, and now he reached inside the bag and pulled out the wristlet. The outside looked okay, but we were more concerned about the contents. I could see the curiosity in Nevers' face; I could also see the worry. We were holding our breath for a miracle, for God to throw us a bone.

"One tube of lipstick. Three hundred dollars in hundreds and twenties. Two keys, one car, one house. And one list. Looks like a 'To Do' list. Arden would you like to do the honors?" asked Jules.

"Sure," I said, pulling on a pair of gloves. "Let's see…Withdraw cash, gas in car, get nails done, call Arceneaux."

"Excuse me? Call who?" asked Nevers.

"It just says 'Arceneaux'. You don't think…"

"I don't know about Nevers, but I do," said Sally. "It explains a lot."

"That harlot! Do you think she was doing him, too?"

"Nevers!" said Jules sternly. I was too busy laughing to be offended. The truth is that Nevers was dead on.

"Well, how else would she have gotten him to cover for her if she pulled it off? Unless…can we check to see if any of the money went to him?"

"Yes, but I gotta reschedule with the judge first. I have to have this information before I go in there," said Jules. And with a dazed look on his face he got up from the table and went to make the call. Poor guy, working with us had to be making him insane. I mean, just when he thinks he has a handle on this thing, some more shit hits the fan. Jules came back a few minutes later and said that Ezra was looking into it. We were all feeling pretty good about it until Gretchen had to go and open her mouth.

"But what if she wasn't going to pay him until everything was settled?"

"Must you rain on my parade?" I asked. "This is the first good news we've had since this thing started."

"I'm sorry Arden. But if the money was a promise and not a reality, it could leave us high and dry," Gretchen said. It is a good thing she is so fetching because otherwise I would have had to slap her face. And truth be told I didn't trust her. It was ridiculous and I knew it, but that's the way it was.

"Can't we check the account she had the money in? Maybe she'd already set up the transfer for a certain day," said Sally.

"We could. Except they froze all the accounts, remember? I can't even touch my own money."

"That's not true," said Gretchen, "I mean, yes, they froze your accounts, but that doesn't mean that I can't get into them. Nevers, you mind if I use your computer, I might incur some overseas charges."

"I think you know the answer to that," said Nevers. And with those words Gretchen left the room.

Me and Nevers and Sally sat at the dining room table and looked at each other. I think Nevers started laughing first.

"Sorry I called your dead wife a harlot."

"Arden, you're a widow. You should be in black," Sally said, referring to my khakis and white un-tucked button down ensemble.

"I could get something new. Some Prada black."

"I think it's a little late for that," said Nevers laughing. It was a good sound, her laughing.

I really felt optimistic at that point. I mean, we kept finding these pieces, and I could see the big puzzle in my minds' eye coming together. Like when you are little and you go to your Grandmother's house, and there on a card table in the living room is this big puzzle, with a smoldering ashtray on one side and depending on what time of day you're there, a scotch on the other. And maybe you climb up in the chair, knowing you are not allowed to touch it, but mentally you start putting the pieces where they go.

You can literally see it coming together.

My Mama had gotten back from France the day before and maybe she'd brought back some particles of a miracle from Lourdes and that's what was making me feel better about the situation. I'm not really sure though, because when she saw me you could tell the 'Mama' in her was worried to death and mad. Not because of what had happened, but because I tried to keep her out of the loop. It's like being a child all over again and doing something stupid like crossing a busy street on your own...they want to spank you and hug you all at the same time. And I knew she wasn't mad; she was just one more of those persons who never cared for Marilyn, and the list was growing longer. At this point I still can't figure out why I married that tramp. Maybe it was because Nevers and I had been at such a turning point in out friendship that I felt I needed someone to take her place. I don't care to analyze it anymore than I have, though.

And I was fuming the day her foster parents called to offer their condolences. They could have told me six months ago that I needed to get out, but they thought maybe this was the real thing for Marilyn. I asked them if they wanted her body for burial, I even offered to pay for it, but the answer was "No". And I couldn't blame them. When it first happened, I figured I'd buy Marilyn a plot and bury her right. But now, well I just didn't know what to do. I really didn't want to be constantly reminded of the fact that my wife wanted to kill me, no matter what we'd had together before she went crazy. And I guess we didn't have all that much.

I didn't feel too bad though. Turns out no one really knew all that much about her, except those damn people who "raised" her. When Gavin called from New York we talked for a long time about Marilyn. He swore he knew nothing about her life, and I believed him. I mean how could he?

He said he thought that she'd slept with some PR guy who used to work for Kelley Publishing, but that in and of itself wasn't something that would make you think she could seriously plot someone's murder. It only made her more of a ...well, you get the picture. It hurt my head to continue thinking about it, so I stopped. Sally had to get back to Jackson and after she left Nevers and I went into the den and lay around like trashy people, just doing nothing.

"How are you feeling?" I asked her. She was lying backwards in the big green chair wishing her hair could still brush the floor.

"I'm okay. Just ready for all of this to be over. I never realized that proving someone's innocence could be such hard work. I mean, really."

"Well, I thank you for all that you've done. Once again you came to my rescue."

"You did it for me last year. Not that I was facing any jail time or anything, but my life would be shit right now of I'd let Stewart get away. And I would have if it weren't for you."

"Nevers you don't give yourself enough credit. You never have. I think you would have done the right thing."

"You want to do something for me? Go get me a beer. I think I'm stuck," she said. So I went to the kitchen and got us a couple of beers. When I came back, she was sitting upright in the chair with a strange look on her face.

"What if what we have isn't enough?" she asked.

"It will be," I said, popping the lids off two beers. I'm not usually a beer drinker, but living with Nevers and Stewart for almost two weeks had changed that. They buy the good stuff. Not to say Nevers doesn't throw back a Budweiser here and there, but for the most part, it is good beer only at The Drive.

"But how do you know it's enough?" she asked.

"Because I do. So quit whining and quit worrying, whore."

"I'm married now," she said, throwing a pillow in my direction, "you can't call me a whore anymore."

"Whatever, whore. Drink your beer and shut-up."

One Month Later

Arden and I were lying out on the wharf, soaking up some sun, drinking some Abita Strawberry Harvest Lager, which was sweet and yummy and perfect for the day. The Kinks' *Give the People What They Want* album was playing in the background. Arden had tried to slip a Britney Spears CD in the changer, but I caught him and as a result he almost lost a hand. Stewart had gone over to the marina to gas up the boat and when he got back we were going to go for a ride.

"Do you know that there are pecan groves in Tucson?" I asked Arden.

"You are lying," he said.

"No, I swear. Just south of the city there are pecan trees all over the place, whole fields of them."

"I don't believe you."

"You are a shit," I said, laughing out loud at his stubbornness. It had been this way since the charges were dropped and Arden got his money back.

That day, when Sally brought the purse in and things started looking good for Arden, he said he knew then that nothing was going to happen, and he ended up being right, which was great, except that he felt it first so there was some smugness involved. He had ensconced himself in the den that afternoon and just sort of let events unfold. I sat there with him, but we didn't do a whole lot of talking. We drank some beer and watched the birds and squirrels in the back yard. I was thinking about all the times we'd been in trouble before. It was all pretty minor. My favorite was the night that the three of us, me, Arden, and Sally got busted for having dinner at the Pioneer Club; if memory serves, we were about eighteen. The Pioneer Club is a restaurant on top of a bank building downtown, and as far as Lake Charles goes, it is somewhat exclusive. Of course we weren't members but we wanted to have dinner there. So we made a reservation in someone else's name.

We dressed to the nines; Arden in a suit, Sally and I in dresses and heels, and we took the elevator to the top and told the Host that we were meeting the person in whose name we'd made the reservation. We had been told that said person was out of town by someone we thought was a reliable source. We were seated in style and treated rather well. Of course it became obvious that the member we were supposed to have dinner with wasn't coming, but we got through half of our entrée before they threw us out. Turns out another party of guests inquired as to who the new members were and when it was explained that we were guests of so and so, those people said, "They're in Jamaica!" It should have been embarrassing, but we acted like we were put out; throwing our napkins on the table and storming out.

And even though we were all of age, our parents were called. That's how it is in Lake Charles.

We hung out in the den until the sun started to go down. When that happened we moved to the front porch. Stewart was already out there in his favorite rocker and Arden joined him. I laid down on the swing which was my perch anyway.

     "What do you think Arden?" asked Stewart.
     "Remember that conversation we had while Nevers was in Tucson?"
     "The one about things we still hadn't done? That one?"
     "Yeah. Well, I know we'd been drinking..."
     "Just a little."

"Yeah, a little. Anyway, here's the deal. The first one we talked about? Going to Italy? We need to go ahead and book that shit."

"You feel that good about things?" asked Stewart.

"I do," was Arden's reply. Then: "Why you don't?" he asked quickly, like he'd gotten ahead of himself.

"Arden, man, here's the deal. Growing up was great for me. I had everything I could ever want. But I never had a brother, and as we all know, Muffy could be a pill sometimes (he looked up at the sky when he said Muffy's name, like he wanted her to know he was joking). When I met you I liked you immediately, which I think is hard to come by. When you warned me that my wife was going to try to make a shambles of what she and I had, I listened. That was good information to have. You've been my brother. You were looking out for me from day one. I've known from the beginning that you didn't hurt Marilyn. If anything, you took too much abuse yourself. And if I thought they were gonna put you in jail you'd already be so far away from here that no one could ever find you." And then Stewart looked at Arden with admiration and Arden gave him the sly smile that said, "I know what you mean."

"God, y'all are cheesy," I said from my perch on the swing and Arden lobbed a lime at me from his drink. They knew, though, that if I hadn't made a joke I'd have been crying, so they let it slide. Besides, Stewart is kind of like the *Silent Bob* to me and Arden's *Jay*. So to hear him say so much to someone other than me was big.

It was a perfect night. We sat on the front porch and talked about stupid shit. Crawfish season, the color of the neighbor's new car ("Tacky," said Arden), and the ingredients of Miss Shirley's Sad Cake. We finally decided to go in and get some sleep, and for the first time in a while I think everyone slept soundly. Of course there was still a chance that Arden would have to go to trial, and I guess that meant there was still a chance that he would have to go to jail, but at that moment it wasn't a reality we believed in.

When Detective Ezra Owens showed up on the front porch the next day, holding Eva's hand in broad daylight, we knew things looked good for Arden. But Ezra didn't have all the scoop on Jules' meeting with ADA Whitman and the judge, so we waited some more. Ezra did tell us that he'd witnessed a confrontation between Sheriff Arceneaux and Miss Lorelei.

"Now I know where you get it," said Ezra.

"Get what?" asked Arden.

"Your attitude, your spunk, whatever you want to call it. I mean to tell you, your Mama was in there letting that man have it."

"I wish I could have witnessed that," I said.

"Not me," said Arden. "I've been there." We all laughed at that.

"Little as she is, she was in that man's face, and I tell you, she was giving him the what-for, pointing her finger at him and admonishing him like a little boy. And you know, that's what he looked like; a kid. He looked scared to death."

"I've been on the other end of that pointed finger; he probably was scared to death," Arden replied with a sigh.

"Well, no matter what they do to him, I don't think it can get much worse that a good talking to from Miss Lorelei," said Sally. And she knew. We'd also been on the receiving end of that pointed finger.

Probably not as bad as Arden, but just enough to know we never wanted to be there again. Sally turned baby Jackson around on her lap and started cooing at him that he was never gonna be so bad, that he was the sweetest boy in the whole world, and we looked at her like she was crazy and laughed again. Sally put Jackson down on the floor then and he took off. For the longest time that baby had no interest in crawling, and then one day he just decided to do it, and he did. My house wasn't necessarily baby-proof, but neither were our mothers' houses when we were babies. Sally wasn't all that concerned.

"So we don't know what happened legally, yet, do we?" I asked, picking up Jackson who had crawled over to me.

"I think I know, but we'll wait for Jules. He'll have all the details," said Ezra.

We decided to make some lunch, so Eva and I headed for the kitchen. I pulled some shrimp out of the freezer and started thawing it in some cold water. Eva got out some bell pepper, onions, and celery and started chopping. I hollered at Sally to come make a roux because even though I was capable, hers was better. Stewart picked Jackson up off the kitchen floor and all the boys headed out to the backyard. Ezra and Arden were smoking and Stewart sat in the grass and played with Jackson, rolling a ball back and forth. Things were looking good. We got the shrimp Creole simmering, and everyone was sitting around the table in the backyard when Jules called to say he was on his way over. Sally and I had been sitting on the swing with Jackson and when we realized he was asleep, Sally went inside to put him down. The rest of us headed in and planted ourselves at the dining room table, once again. That table was really some of the best money ever spent.

We sat there quietly, waiting for Jules, a lullaby playing softly over the baby monitor. The first thing we heard was the sound of tires on the gravel driveway. We knew Jules couldn't pull too far in because of Sally and Ezra's cars. Then we heard the car door, and his footsteps heading toward the walkway to the front porch. He knocked softly on the screen door.

"Come on in, Jules. The screen door is unlocked," said Stewart. And we heard him pull open the screen door. "We're in the dining room."

"Why is it so damn quiet?" asked Jules. "I've been around you people for almost two weeks now and I've never heard it this quiet." The first thing we saw when he came into the room was his smile; those white teeth set against that cocoa skin. We all waited with bated breath for him to say something else.

"So, what's it gonna be? Am I packing for prison?" asked Arden.

"Not for this bullshit," said Jules with a devious grin. And we all started screaming. Screaming and hugging and laughing and crying. Poor Jules and Ezra caught up in our moment of pure joy, they had no idea what hit them.

"So what happened?" asked Sally.

"Well, let me give you the short version…With Ezra's help, the Sheriff's Department uncovered the deal put together by Marilyn and Arceneaux. Seems the two of them ran into each other at Fred's in Big Lake one night. One thing leads to another and you got yourself a murder plot. The whole thing started to unravel when Ezra found out about Miss Lorelei dating Arceneaux in high school. When Sally found the purse with the "To Do" list in it and we checked bank records we found that there was a transfer set up for the day after the planned murder. Of course the money never got moved because

Marilyn had to be the one to authorize it. This pissed the Sheriff off something awful. Between that and the old crap about Miss Lorelei ruining his football career, he went after Arden."

"I don't get it though. Why would he risk his career for all this?" I asked.

"The sex," answered Arden before Jules had a chance to.

"Come, on," said Stewart in disbelief.

"Really. It made me stupid for a year of my life. It made the bank guy do highly illegal things, *in the bank*. And it played a part in Sheriff Arceneaux losing his career by plotting to kill someone. I mean sure, there was money involved, but the sex is always what sealed the deal for her. It was her power, her upper hand. No pun intended," Arden explained.

"He's right," said Jules. "To hear these guys tell it, they were totally manipulated by sex. Although it'll get laughed right out of court if they use it as part of a defense. They didn't want to admit to it at all, but I knew the right things to ask after talking to Arden. She was a good old fashioned vixen."

"They're taking this to trial?" Sally asked.

"I doubt it. They'll both probably plead out. They know what kind of circus it would be if it went that far," Jules said.

"So it's over," said Arden softly.

"Yes, my friend, you may have your life back. All charges have been dropped and your money will be back in your account within ten days. I would suggest switching banks, though."

"That will be my pleasure," said Arden. "To waltz in there and tell them to stick their whole bank right in their puss. Mmmm hmmm, they won't be getting any business from anyone I know for a long time."

"I don't think they'll be getting any business from anyone at all. Ever," I said. "And it serves them right. Never hire anyone who can be corrupted by sex."

"Well, I'm going to call Jack," said Sally.

"Shit, just start calling everybody," said Stewart happily. He felt the same thing I felt at that moment, and I loved him even more for it. But it was already too late for calling everyone we knew. Word travels fast in a town the size of Lake Charles and during the hour or so since Jules left the courthouse, word was already out. God bless the South.

Getting Back To Normal
(or at least our version of it)

Within days everyone in town knew what had gone on between Sheriff Arceneaux and Marilyn. Needless to say, Arceneaux was no longer the Sheriff. He had fallen from his position in the most disgraceful way, like poop from a bird's behind. It was great. And he was facing some serious jail time for conspiracy to commit, even though Arden wasn't dead. Ezra had gone down to Fred's and talked to some regulars about Arceneaux and said people couldn't believe it when they saw the Sheriff for Calcasieu Parish practically getting it on with "some young floozy" at the bar. Apparently spit swapping was not something they were used to witnessing on a regular basis.

The bank guy, Elliot Reyes was also facing jail time for some form of fraud. And some charge for exposing himself. Even though no one saw it, it must have been against the law for him to take out his business so Marilyn could get down to business, right there inside the bank. To tell you the truth, I didn't really care, as long as Arden came out clean, which he did. And no one held it against him that his wife was a conniving slut. We had fun for a few days, granting interviews and telling our side of the story. We heard all kinds of stories about Marilyn after that, guys came out of the woodwork. None of them were approached about committing murder, but plenty of them were approached for raunchy sex. I could tell that this bothered Arden to a certain extent, but I reminded him, once again, that she was trash and we were better off leaving her at the curb where she belonged, with the other garbage. It was my way of saying it wasn't worth it; to worry about her that is. To me, Marilyn wasn't worth the effort.

Since we had too much class to sell pictures of a dead woman to *Hustler* we built a fire in the pit in the backyard and had a ceremonial burning. There was no way we were going to hold on to pictures which were taken in such bad taste. Later, Arden brought his housekeeper back in and she scrubbed his house from top to bottom; Sally and I went in and got rid of everything associated with Marilyn and we told the Sheriff's Department to dispose of anything they'd already seized. Arden still didn't know where his boots were, but I kept reassuring him and he would let up for a few days and then we'd go through the process again.

The afternoon that found us waiting on the wharf for Stewart was also a big day. We had decided we needed some rest, number one, and number two…well, we had a job to do.

"Where is that husband of yours?" Arden asked after Abita number four.

"Who knows. Probably having a beer with Grant at the marina. He'll be here, don't worry."

"I'm ready to get the show on the road, dammit. I'm sick of looking at this thing."

"Yeah, it is kinda ugly. What are you going to do with it after you empty the contents?"

"Throw it in the lake."

"Arden, don't you think there's enough shit in this lake already?"

"Yes, but at least this won't give anybody cancer," he laughed. And then I laughed, and then it got stupid. Back in the screened off room behind us the CD changer spit out a different tune. So by the time my husband did show up Arden and I were belting out Little Big Town's *Boondocks*, and we were feeling it after all that Abita. That song is like an anthem for most people raised in the South.

"Y'all look like a bunch of damn fools from out in the middle of the lake, you know that don't you?"

"We suffer for our art," said Arden putting our cooler of yummy strawberry lager on the boat.

"Besides," I said, "you married us."

"That I did," laughed Stewart. "That I did." I was altogether taken with him once more. I always loved him a little more when he was in his element, and something about him on that boat, his backward baseball cap with the blonde hair sticking out from underneath and the obnoxious Oakley sunglasses that I hated, well, it moved me. So did the way he offered his hand when I climbed aboard. I couldn't help it, I porn kissed him right there.

"Enough with the PDA," said Arden. "Let's groove tonight."

So we headed out. Off to one of the small islands nestled in our chemical filled lake. There are a few of these islands around, and they are not what you think. There are no beautiful palms surrounded by flowing water and exotic birds; no. Our islands are just pieces of land scattered here and there on a great man-made lake. A little sand, maybe some grass. Nothing special. But from our lake you can get to other waters, waters which were used for running goods, stolen or otherwise, back when this was new territory. And this is where we thought Marilyn deserved to be. Her ashes scattered among the ghosts of the pirates who once ruled the waters around us. When we thought we had found the perfect place, Stewart stopped the boat and we climbed out, onto the soggy shore. We'd gotten a little rain the night before and things were still pretty damp, but we weren't sinking in the mud, which was good.

We stood there for a moment, the mosquitoes swarming with a gusto I'd never witnessed, while Stewart squared things away with the boat. The slapping of limbs going on between Arden and I was comical to say the least. It just never crossed our minds to wear bug repellent to a funeral. Arden finally said, "I guess this spot will do." It wasn't like a scene from a movie where the urn-emptier runs along the shore of some fabulous beach releasing the ashes in such a way to portray the spirit of life flowing back into the universe. None of that poetry for us. Arden simply turned the urn over and the ashes fell out into one gray pile. It looked like someone had sat there in the sand and smoked a million cigarettes. I stifled a laugh. I wanted to be serious, but the way Arden did things never ceased to amuse me.

"I guess I should say something," he said.

"That would be appropriate," said Stewart softly.

"The only problem is, I don't know what to say." This was strange. Arden is almost never without comment.

"Just say what you feel," I told him.

"You don't want me to do that."

"Look, it's just me and Stewart. You can say what you need to say. We won't judge you, you know that."

"Okay," he said, taking a deep breath. "Marilyn. I don't know why you did the things you did. Some people, including you, may think that I am hateful, but I did love you in the beginning. You had a drive that I had never experienced before and I found it exhilarating. But then you changed. You started to hurt me, you were hateful to my friends and my Mama, but I still thought we could work it out. That day, the day we went down to the Creole Nature Trail, I thought you were making an effort. I turns out you were only trying to hurt me again. I don't know where you ended up, but as long as I don't ever have to look at your face again, I have to say, I really don't care where it is…This is stupid."

"No it's not, Arden."

"Yes it is, Nevers. I really don't have anything to say about her, or to her. She was a trashy whore and I'm glad she's gone. There. I'm done. Anybody want another lager?"

And with that, the ceremony was over. We got back into the boat and true to his word Arden threw the urn over the side. And just like that we were done with Marilyn. The only thing I ever heard Arden say about her after that is that she disgraced one of the best names out there. "She should be ashamed." Stewart took a couple spins around the lake before heading home and by the time we got back our spirits had been lifted. I don't know why this place makes me happy. But I do love it. Here's the thing about Lake Charles...When Arden and I wrote our book, no one took much interest that is, until it hit *The New York Times* best seller list. After it hit the *Times* someone at the local paper finally decided to review it.

Even though just about everybody in town had read it, mostly out of curiosity, you know to see if they were in it, the city didn't jump behind it until someone bigger did. And that is the thing with Lake Charles. You've got to hit the REALLY big time, or you're just still someone from here. Maybe they thought the book would shame them, who knows? But I thought of all this while we were headed back to the house. It's amazing what drama will bring out in a city. The day of Marilyn's demise the phone rang off the hook. The day the cops issued their warrant and searched the house the local television station was there. And then we're back at the reality television argument. Write a best-selling book; well, let's wait and see what *The New York Times* has to say first.

As for my feelings about Marilyn…Well, I can honestly say that I didn't hate her in the beginning. Sure I had my doubts, but that's normal when your best friend marries someone you don't really know. But then, Arden married her and he didn't know a whole lot more about her than we did. As for the whole growing up in a foster home and not remembering her parents, well that's where my mean streak comes out.

I don't believe that people should use abuse or neglect or things like that as excuses. You know, the whole, "My Daddy used to spank me and that's why I bludgeoned my girlfriend to death" defense. Marilyn could say that she had a hard life; that she slept with older men for money, but those were decisions, not choices. And my response to that would have been, "Get a job. McDonald's is always hiring." It is a theory that doesn't go over well in polite society. Which is okay because I've never belonged there.

Even though the day had brought up some stuff that none of us liked thinking about, it had still been a good day. Riding in the boat always soothed my soul, and even though my hair was getting a little longer, it still wasn't long enough to tangle, which was a plus. We got back to the wharf and Stewart and Arden unloaded the boat. "The load is lighter," Arden said, and we laughed. We knew what he meant. While the guys carried the ice chest and other assorted crap back to the house, I went inside to straighten up. I sorted bottles and cans for my Mama who still insisted upon driving them to Jennings for recycling. She will one day save the world single handedly.
I had just crossed the street when I heard Arden call out…

"What, pray tell, is this?"

"What is what?" I asked.

"This box addressed to you from some shoe place in Houston. It seems to have appeared here by magic while we were gone."

"Not magic. UPS."

"Give it up Nevers."

"Where is my husband?"

"In the shower. Now quit stalling. Did you have my boots resoled? Because I might be mad if you did that. I love those boots, they are perfect the way they are."

"No I didn't and you can't open the box until Sally's here, so quit whining. I'm going to call her. Go get in the shower." He glared at me like a scolded child and then yanked open the screen door and stormed inside. I went to call Sally, and then I joined my husband in the shower.

It had been a quiet day, but strange too. I couldn't think about Arden dumping those ashes again without laughing. And yes, that's wrong, but it was unavoidable. Seriously, if someone had told me a month ago that someone was going to die and I was going to be glad I wouldn't have believed it. Even when Muffy died, I was still sad. The loss of human life is monumental. And I think I justified my feelings by thinking if it hadn't been Marilyn, it would have been Arden and then I would have had to kill Marilyn myself. And although it wouldn't have been easy, I think I could have done it. Not on my own of course, I'm not a mafia boss or anything...you know, don't cross me, but come on. Jail wouldn't have been enough for her.

I think everyone feels that way too, they just don't admit it. Maybe I'm wrong, but I don't think so. I was just glad I didn't have to think about any of it anymore. This scandal was over and that was fine with me. Any more drama and I might have had to lose my mind, seriously, we needed a break.

Alligator Shoes

By the time Sally and her crew arrived, Stewart and Arden and I were sitting out back, drinking cold iced tea with lemon, a little Shakira playing in the background. Stewart and Arden were quite taken with Shakira. She was still growing on me.

"What's up y'all? How'd the thing go today?"

"It was right up your alley. Wish you could have been there," said Arden while kissing Sally's cheek and taking Jackson from her in one seamless move.

"Jack, there's beer in the fridge in the garage. Help yourself," Stewart said. He enjoyed my rule that if you come to my house you should feel comfortable enough to get your own stuff. Not that I didn't enjoy playing hostess, but sometimes you gotta take a break. Jack offered to get Sally a beer, but she declined, explaining that Jackson is cutting teeth and not sleeping very well.

"Okay, she's here. Can we open the damn box?" Arden asked.

"Wait 'til Jack gets back from the garage," I said. "And then you can open the box, petulant child." Arden started to hand off Jackson to me, but he was ready to move and groove, so Sally took him and put him down in the grass. We laughed as he took off in search of plant life, or worse yet, bugs to sample. Arden was hovering over the box when Jack came around the corner, beer in hand.

"Took you long enough," he said. And then he went to work with the little Swiss Army knife I'd given him for high school graduation. I watched his face as he opened the box. He was puzzled at first, and then you could see the click of recognition. The smile of understanding what we'd done. And knowing his other boots weren't lost.

"You are kidding me," he said. "How in the hell did you pull this one off?"

"Sally and I did it together. In fact there should be a couple more boxes in there. One has your old boots in it. Since I didn't have a mold of your foot, I sent in the old boots so they had something to go on." I pulled the box toward me so I could dole out the rest of the gifts. A pair of snappy slides for Sally, with a beautiful band of alligator just below the toe. The boys got belts; Stewart, Jack and even Jules. I didn't know if Jules would wear his, but I knew he'd understand the gesture. And for me, a beautiful pair of backless, open-toed pumps with a nice heel, made from a mold of my foot.

"Who did you say made this stuff?" asked Jack.

"This place in Houston, on Caplin. And the guy came highly recommended."

"And he should be," said Arden holding his leg out in front of him to better admire the boot on his foot. "Highly recommended, that is. They feel just like the old ones, they are so soft."

"The pumps are too," I said, standing up so I could walk around in mine. They were stunning and made my legs look great. "Sally?"

"Honey, these slides are never coming off my feet," she replied. "How did he get the hide so soft?"

"It's one of his secrets. I don't know how he does it, but that's why he's in demand."

"The belt is great," said Stewart. "I'll be able to wear it with everything." Jack agreed. Sitting out in the backyard, trying on alligator accessories. It could have been Christmas.

"I still don't understand how y'all did this," said Arden,

"It was an experience, I'll tell you that," said Sally. "And that old man, Mr. Trahan, he is quite the business man."

"It was fun. Jack located the guy who took out the alligator and we went to see him. There was an exchange of goods, so to speak. And voila! Alligator accessories all around," I explained.

"Did y'all tell him who you were?"

"Arden, we're smarter than that. And anyway, he swore to forget us," I said.

"And he did. You know that's where I found the purse, right?"

"You're kidding? You never said anything about that," said Stewart.

"Well, I didn't want to get into it with Jules, even though Gretchen was with me. But when we couldn't find it at the Sheriff's office, I kept thinking about where it could have disappeared to. And the only logical explanation was that it had gone into the alligator with her," Sally explained.

"Apparently it got lodged in the throat of the beast and Mr. Trahan, being the entrepreneur that he is, held on to it," I summed up.

"And as usual, he parted with it, for a price," said Sally. "I told y'all he was good."

Arden laughed and said, "So how much are y'all into this guy for?"

"You don't want to know," said Sally and I in unison. We all laughed at that. We had doled out quite a bit for the hide. But the purse being found was priceless, you couldn't even put a tag on it.

We sat around for a while longer, enjoying the outdoors. Summer would be creeping up soon enough, and when that happened, you could only be outside and comfortable between the hours of 10 pm and 7am. We were trying to decide on what to do for dinner when Kiki and Wes rounded the corner from the garage side of the house. They were both wearing black t-shirts with white writing that said, "RPM's…Where everyday is Rex Manning day." I started cracking up immediately. Wes and Kiki knew that *Empire Records* was one of my favorite movies, and they had gotten hooked on it as well; incorporating things from the movie into everyday life at the shop. They could exercise music vetos on each other, and me while I was there, and Wes often wore a name tag that read: Warren.

When I noticed that Kiki was carrying a bag, I thought, "What now?" But it turns out that they had brought t-shirts for everybody. There were even some in there for Jules and Ezra. "Just a little something to show our appreciation," said Wes.

"Your appreciation for what?" I asked.

"For having a great boss," said Kiki.

"But she's never there," said Arden.

"I was just thinking the same thing," Sally threw in.

"Thanks, y'all. But really, why the t-shirts?"

"Well, even though you've been out a lot lately, we still think you are a great boss. And you've given us a great place to work," said Kiki.

"Yeah, you trust us to run the store and you don't give us any shit," Wes explained.

"Well said," Stewart laughed. "Throw me one of those t-shirts, Mister." And so Wes took hold of the bag and started throwing out t-shirts like it was Mardi Gras. And of course we all put them on. With our alligator accessories.

We had to take two cars to dinner that night. Tony's had been the clear winner because everyone could find something on the menu and the staff would accommodate our obnoxiousness. It felt good to get out. Arden had ventured into a couple of places, but we hadn't done something this public yet. I had called Eva and she and Ezra showed up. And of course there were already people there we knew. It turned into an impromptu party. I'm sure there were still people around who thought Arden was guilty of something, but I'd say that 99% of Lake Charles believed he was innocent, and because of that people kept coming to the table to shake his hand or offer a kind word. Even Adonis came out from behind his post at the register to say congratulations. Things were finally starting to feel normal.

Within the next week I was back at work. Not quite full-time, but I did show up every day. It was fun to be back in the swing of things. Kiki and Wes had made their "Rex Manning" t-shirts their uniform and it was a great addition to the shop, especially because you never knew how they were going to accessorize.

Business was good, schools were on the verge of letting out and we had more evening traffic. A couple of people came into apply for summer jobs, but I wasn't sure if I needed them. Wes did talk me into hiring one girl by the name of Lorraine, as in quiche, who was a strawberry blonde with the biggest brown eyes you've ever seen. We liked her immediately. She was a little quiet at first, but eventually came into her own, realizing that even though it's not listed, quick wit was part of the job description.

Lorraine had an abundance of knowledge when it came to music. Like me she'd been raised on everything under the sun. Her familiarity with genres from show tunes to metal was impressive. Her crush on Wes was obvious. And it was mutual, which gave Kiki all kinds of new material. She'd put on cheesy love songs, including, but not limited to, the Beach Boys' *God Only Knows*, and tease them relentlessly.

Wes and Lorraine took it in stride. Lorraine, who was from Beaumont, Texas, was from a big family and discovered quickly enough that she had just extended it. Once she figured that out, the teasing was nothing. It was fun having someone new in the shop and it was fun watching Kiki mother hen the way I did. Lorraine also won points with me when she admitted to loving the movie *Dogma*. You can't work in my shop if you don't like Kevin Smith. Sure, it's discrimination, but who gives a shit.

It was a couple of Friday's later when Eva walked into the shop, a huge grin on her face. She was glowing. Of course the first thing that went through my mind was that she was pregnant. But the huge grin turned sly on me when I looked at her more closely. It was silent as I gave her the once over from head to toe. It wasn't until I made the second pass that I noticed the ring on her finger. I guess I'm losing my touch. Normally that would have been the first thing I looked for. No one else saw it though, and for a moment Eva and I shared a knowing look. Eye to eye. We understood what was going on, what it meant. And it was such an incredible moment for us. And then she finally said it.

"I'm getting married!!!" And for a moment we were all silent.

"No way," shouted Kiki. "Oh, shit Eva. Y'all are gonna have the most beautiful babies." And we all laughed. But it was true. Ezra was quite a piece of work. But nothing compared to Eva.

"Good, Lord Kiki, don't rush me. I just got proposed to last night," said Eva with a weary sigh.

"Last night? When were you planning on telling us?" asked Wes.

"Well, I couldn't quite get to the phone last night," said Eva grinning again.

"How did he do it?" asked Lorraine.

"Please tell me he didn't ask you during sex," I said.

"Now Nevers, you know he has more class than that. He asked me at Wal-Mart."

"Wal-Mart?" shouted Wes. "And that's classy?"

"It was the way he did it. We were there buying groceries…"

"And we all know how romantic groceries are," said Kiki.

"Are y'all gonna listen?"

"We're shutting up," I said, giving my 'kids' the evil eye.

"Okay, so we're shopping for groceries so we could cook dinner, and we're talking and cutting up. And he turns to me and says, "I want to do this with you for the rest of my life." And I said what? Come to Wal-Mart? And he says, "No. I want to cook dinner with you every night for the rest of our lives." And I knew he could tell I didn't understand, so he gets down on one knee in the bakery section, in front of the French bread display, and pulls the box out of his pocket and asks me to marry him. Of course there was a crowd, and people were clapping. You know Wal-Mart. And then he slips the ring on my finger and just looks at me."

"And of course you say "yes." Right? I mean you wouldn't be standing here with the ring on if you didn't say "yes," Kiki asks.

"Of course I said yes. Wouldn't you?"

"Hell, yeah," said Kiki laughing. She'd been the first to lay eyes on that man, and even I could admit to him being a piece of work in the looks department.

"Congratulations, honey," I said, hugging Eva.

"You know what this means?" asked Wes. "We get to have a big ole party. Hot damn!"

"And I'll throw it," I said. It was the least I could do. Eva and I were not just cousins, and she'd been with me through so much. And she deserved the best, as did Ezra. He had risked his job to help out with the investigation and for that we would always be grateful. Becoming family for real was just the next step. I insisted upon opening a bottle of champagne then, so we could celebrate. And yes, I keep one in the fridge at the shop. You just never know.

A Moment In The Sun

God things were going well. I kept waiting for the other shoe, the one made of alligator hide, to drop. That's how it is with us. One day we're flying high, the next day someone's getting mauled to death by an alligator. With Arden out from under his cloud of suspicion, we felt free again. Free to get out and do things that we hadn't gotten to do while he was facing charges for killing Marilyn. From start to finish it was only about three weeks, but it felt like a lifetime. And when it was over the days started to fly by again. And since Arden had gone back to his house ours felt quiet and lifeless. Which wasn't a bad thing, really. I needed the rest, and Stewart made sure I got it. But there is always that itch in me that needs to get scratched. So about a week after Arden went back to his house, I rounded up the usual suspects for a weekend of fun in New Orleans.

We were about a month away from Eva's engagement party, which gave me time to have some fun before we got down to the business of planning and throwing that shindig. The wedding was set for October, one of the most beautiful months in Louisiana. And while we'd been prepping for that, I'd kind of put the party on the back burner. It was still gonna go down, but we decided to wait until a few people, some friends of Ezra's, could get here. He was without family, not unlike Stewart had been, and that brought the two of them closer. They'd been fishing a lot lately. Sometimes I'd go and just hang out on the boat and read; other times I'd stay behind and hang out with Arden. No matter how much you crave it, solitude can get boring. And I believed that Arden had had just about enough. I know he had to come to terms with what happened, he was feeling guilty even though he did nothing wrong, but there comes a time when you have to start sucking it up and get back in the game.

I pushed a little, and that's all it took. He was ready to quit wallowing. A weekend in New Orleans was what we all needed. We were going to miss Jack (who was staying behind with Jackson so Sally could go and cut loose), but the morning we left, Me, Stewart, Sally, and Arden, all piled into my Mini Cooper convertible, we knew that it was what we needed more than anything. Of course I made Stewart take the River Road, as it is my favorite way to go. It's more real to me than driving on I-10 and seeing all the outlet malls and other testimonies to commerce. It's not that I'm not a fan of change, but sometimes you gotta give it a rest. My brother Dunham was kind enough to let us stay at his house for the weekend. We just weren't in the mood for a hotel and Dunham has this great little place uptown on Sixth Street. It is a fabulous piece of property with a beautiful yard and even a little lap pool. And it has a garage, off street parking, which is hard to come by in most neighborhoods. Stewart and I talked often of buying the house if Dunham ever decided to sell.

Location is all in New Orleans, and we were happy to be where we were. We poured through the sidewalk gate when we got there, and relaxed immediately. Dunham suggested lunch but none of us felt like getting back in the car, so we sent Dunham, and Arden ended up going after losing three rounds of paper, rock, scissors. We ate lunch by the pool and got Dunham caught up on everything going on at home.

"Y'all made the papers here, you know. Any time there is corruption involved the *Picayune* picks up the story," Dunham explained. "Not that we don't have enough corruption here. Maybe it makes them feel better when shit goes on somewhere else."

"That makes sense. But with Nagin in office you wouldn't think they'd run out of filler," said Sally.

"Shocking, I know, that they would have to look elsewhere, when the murder rate is higher now that he's in office. There are little kids, nine and ten, stealing cars in this neighborhood," said Dunham. I could tell he was a little disgusted.

"Anyway," I said. I didn't want to get caught up in the politics of New Orleans, and if Sally and Dunham got going it could last all night. Louisiana is known for having more corruption in it's government than normal, I didn't think we needed to debate that. "What are the plans for tonight?" I asked.

"Well, Miles is in town, some kind of convention, and his boss put him up downtown. So we gotta go down to the Royal Orleans and pick him up. But after that it's up to y'all," said Dunham.

"I want to go to that bar where the horses come in," said Stewart, "that sounds pretty cool."

"Le Booze," said Arden.

"That's the name of it?" asked Stewart.

"Yep. So obviously it is the place for us," I said.

"Anybody want a Bushwhacker?" asked Dunham. He was the master at mixing the perfect Bushwhacker. They tasted just like the ones you got at The Dock in Pensacola.

"Absolutely," was the answer that came from the peanut gallery.

We sat out back at Dunham's, drinking Bushwhackers and telling outrageous stories. By the time we left to head downtown we were pretty well lit. I thought maybe the walk to the street car would sober us up a little, but that wasn't in the cards. When we got down to

St. Charles, we opted for a van cab, because the street cars were running full. Damn tourists. We ended up sharing with two women from Michigan who were just headed to Houston's. All the damn restaurants in New Orleans and they were going to a chain. But the joke was on them, because when the got out of the cab, one of them left their purse. It wasn't discovered, however, until we'd gotten past Lee Circle. And then Arden said, "Wah, Wah, Wah," in his best *Peanuts* voice. We all started laughing so hard that I thought the driver was gonna drop us off in the middle of the road. Instead he left us at the corner of Canal and Carondelet.

We hoofed it the rest of the way to the hotel, stopping to get a drink on the way. The Royal Orleans is fairly classy, so Dunham went up by himself to get his friend Miles. He should have been more concerned about leaving us in the lobby. Arden and I discovered a piano tucked away in a hidden alcove and a round of Heart and Soul ensued. It wasn't to be, however. Just when we got the rhythm right, and convinced Sally to sing for us, a hulking, tree trunk looking security guard closed the show. No encore, no nothing. We were a little bitter. Dunham was relieved that he missed the recital, and as soon as he and Miles came down, we headed out. Miles is from England and so much fun to go out with. The first time I hung out with him, we were down on Bourbon Street and he kept saying he was "pissed." And we kept trying to figure out why he was mad. In our drunken state, we were unaware that 'pissed' in England is sloppy drunk in the states.

We headed to Le Booze, where of course we took over the bar. Dancing and singing and general stupidity reigned. We fed the horses when the cops brought them in. They don't come all the way in, they are too big for that, but they do come about halfway and it is amusing to say the least. Especially if there is someone in the bar who doesn't know what's going on.

At some point, after too much to drink, Arden took Sally and I aside. We knew what was coming, but we let him speak. We knew the outcome would be worse if we tried to shut him up.

"I just want y'all to know that I know I couldn't have gotten through this without y'all. I mean mentally, we all know I was a total wreck, especially those first couple of days. But not only did you take care of me, you made me laugh. And we all know how important that is," he said. To say Arden was a little drunk would have been an understatement. He was getting mushy in public, which is not his style. Sally, however, was getting impatient. Which was exactly her style. Even sober.

"So why aren't we laughing now?" she asked.

"Because I needed to let y'all know how I feel," Arden explained.

"But, Arden, we know how you feel. You feel drunk," I said, and Sally started laughing hysterically.

"Y'all are a bunch of bitches. You know that?"

"But we're your bitches. What could be better?" I asked.

"Nothing in the world as far as I'm concerned,' said Sally.

"And you are our bitch too, honey. And us bitches gotta stick together," I said.

"Well, if I get to be a bitch too then I guess it's okay," said Arden.

"Honey, you've always been the biggest bitch of all," said Sally, which caused her to get slapped, but we were laughing which is what everyone wanted.

We spent the rest of the weekend relaxing and eating. Our friend Lola ("from Nola," as Arden would say) came by the second night and ending up cooking for us. It was then that we discovered that Lola not only knew all there was to know about the people and places in New Orleans, she also knew all there was to know about the food. The crawfish pies were exceptional.

Sunday morning Arden and I rode the street car down to get beignets at Café du Monde. There was always a risk that half a bag would be gone by the time we got back to the house so we got three dozen.

"Let's buy a place down here," I said.

"Sho nuff, honey. I'm sure Lola knows somebody in real estate. We could go in together if y'all want."

"I'd love that. You and I could have so much fun decorating. Let's start with the Sunday paper and see what kind of market there is."

"Sounds like a plan."

Stewart was up to the task too. It seemed strange that I would be owning two homes, but to Stewart it was no big deal. And he loved New Orleans. Dunham actually knew the right people and we started the ball rolling. I had the feeling we'd be spending a lot more time in New Orleans until we found something, which was a good thing.

The drive home that evening was quiet. I took the wheel and figured since it was going to get dark on me that the interstate was my best bet. By the time we got to the LaPlace exit all my passengers were asleep. But I had my Coke, and a full pack of smokes, so I was good. I felt a little guilty for the cigarettes, but they can't be any worse than what you breathe in on a normal Lake Charles day. I put on a little Bob Schneider and tried not to sing too loud. I played *Metal & Steel* three times and thought about the lyrics. It was one more song that fit our situation. I mean we worked hard to find humor in the wretched situation we were in, but there were times when we just had to deal with things without getting emotional, which for us could be difficult. Because really, what happened to Arden, that whole situation was like being lost without a damn map; most of the time we had no idea which way was up.

When I thought about all Arden and I had been through, so much of it brought on by sheer stupidity, I was proud to have been there for him through this. His thanks were not even necessary. And I realized that what Sally had told me way back when in Nantucket, about us being there for each other even when our lives change, was true. She was a lifeline for me after my surgery. She knew that having baby Jackson around would help me even when some people thought it was the worst thing Sally could ever do, bringing that baby around. And Stewart. My twenty-four-hour-around-the-clock-keep-me-sane-husband. In the middle of the night, first thing in the morning, and those times I couldn't be in the room with my friends because I was so scared for them…Stewart was there.

The sun was setting as I drove over the "*Plié*" and "*Relevé*" bridges. I don't remember for sure who came up with those names for the Atchafalaya Spillway, but it was fitting, their grace always reminding me that Louisiana may be flat in most places, but it is never boring. The state I come from never ceases to amaze me with its beauty and its kindness. Having lived other places, both West and North, I wouldn't trade the complexities of Louisiana's history and government, or the people and the land for anything under the sun.

Maybe it was the sunset. But at that moment I said a little prayer, asking God to watch over the people in the car with me. Asking Him to keep them safe, as much for me as for them. I asked God to watch over everyone I loved, and that was quite a list. But implacable girl that I am, I figured He owed me one. I felt good in that moment; better than I have in a while. And me and Bob and God, we made it home in record time.

This book cannot be dedicated to just one person. It's just not possible. But there are a few people who need to be mentioned...

My husband James, for one. On a day to day basis he supports me more than anyone. He knows when I'm full of crap, and pushes me past the doubt. I love him for that.

Kathryn Quinn Filo. From over 1000 miles away, she orchestrated my first book signing and a launch party and because of her the entire weekend was a success. I can never repay her for those things. She lights a fire under my ass. Thank you, honey.

Charles Mullin...I couldn't have shared this success with anyone else. You've told me more stories over the years, and used more phrases...let's just say I owe a little of my writing style to you.

My Mama, Kathryn Smith Ward. For spiritual support, not just in this endeavor, but for the past 36 years. You've always been my biggest fan.

Clay, Billy, Norman, Claire, and Becca. Y'all word-of-mouthed me to death, and have always been a source of inspiration. I love each and every one of you.

And by name, for many other things: Suzanne LaBove, Brigitte Pulido, Michele Damato, Amy Green Brown, Justin Kase, Quanda Dixon, Suzanne Smith, Marilyn Smith Fulton, and my in-laws Jim, Maryann, and Jennifer (y'all didn't know what you were getting into with me!). And for my West Coast Girls, Lisa and Marisela; y'all keep me sane and entertained!

Last but not least, to my children Austin and Stella. The two of you have enriched my life in ways I never thought possible. I love you more than any words can say! Remember to always dream big!

www.ingramcontent.com/pod-product-compliance
Lightning Source LLC
Chambersburg PA
CBHW032143020726
47496CB00003B/686